Janet was an unwilling eavesdropper

She had watched the woman come out of the car and survey the base building, a strange expression on her face as she stepped up onto the veranda.

She didn't seem to notice Janet in her half-hidden corner. And suddenly Clifford Ransome stepped through the door.

"Clifford!" the woman spoke breathlessly.

"I heard your voice," he said stiffly. Janet couldn't escape the conversation that followed. From the way they talked to each other it was clear that they had been lovers. It was also clear that the woman, at least, was determined that they continue.

Why should Janet find this new knowledge so appalling? "I'm not falling in love with him," she thought helplessly. "I can't be. Especially not now. I ought to despise him."

Lilian Darcy lives in Sydney, Australia. Along with writing romances, she works on scripts for the theater, film and television. Her other interests include winter sports, music and French. She says she writes doctor-nurse romances because it gives her the opportunity to create heroines who are real, who work for their living, care about what they do and lead interesting and fulfilling lives. Although she has no medical training, she has many friends in the profession who delight in providing her with details, even arguing over the exact treatment her hero ought to prescribe!

Flying Doctor

Lilian Darcy

Harlequin Books

TORONTO • NEW YORK • LONDON
AMSTERDAM • PARIS • SYDNEY • HAMBURG
STOCKHOLM • ATHENS • TOKYO • MILAN

Original hardcover edition published in 1986
by Mills & Boon Limited

ISBN 0-373-17027-0

Harlequin Romance first edition December 1988

CHAPTER ONE

It was comparatively cool in the specially-equipped Piper Chieftain aircraft that operated from the Benanda Royal Flying Doctor Service Base. Flying at eight and a half thousand feet, Dr Clifford Ransome and his pilot Bill Kirkley had a magnificent view of the desert's arid beauty. Last night the pair had been up until four in the morning with an emergency flight. Now they were returning to Benanda Base after a day of routine yet tiring clinic flights, and Clifford looked forward with quiet anticipation to the time a few hours hence when he would be able to relax in an easy chair on his screened-in verandah, enjoying the cool of the evening air before an early night.

There would be the city papers to catch up on, and a long brandy-and-dry tinkling with ice would sit on a coffee table beside him. He would be alone. No one to make demands, his own master. He could scarcely wait . . .

At that moment, his pleasant reverie was interrupted by the sound of the aeroplane radio crackling into life. Bill reached out a tanned and weatherbeaten hand to the controls, flipped a switch and gave the correct call-sign.

'Yes, Base, this is Air-Doctor One, reading you.'

Dr Paul Adams' voice came distant but distinct from the speaker.

'Just letting you know I'm about to get on my way to the 'Hill to collect our new nurse. Anything you want while I'm there?'

Bill flipped the switch and was about to speak again when Dr Ransome put out a quick hand to interrupt him.

'Hang on, Bill, what's our position at the moment?'

Bill gave the co-ordinates quickly, then read the doctor's thoughts and added: 'Yes, you're right. It would be quicker for us to go, rather than getting out the second aircraft.'

'And safer. If there's an emergency further North while both planes are in this sector . . .'

'Pardon? You'll have to speak up.' Paul Adams' voice came through the equipment again.

'Sorry, Paul.' This time it was Clifford Ransome who spoke into the radio device. 'We're just discussing a better plan. We're not far from Broken Hill ourselves. We'll get the Green girl.'

'Oh. Right. Yes, if you're in that sector, I suppose. Anyway, you're the boss.'

The disappointment and annoyance in Paul Adams' voice could be heard clearly even through the rough medium of the radio waves. Clifford smiled grimly and Bill let out a frank chuckle, flipping off the communication switch hastily before the sound broke from his lips.

'Looks like Paul's up to the same old tricks,' he said.

Clifford saw the funny side of it too, but couldn't take the matter quite as lightly as Bill did. In his capacity as pilot, Bill Kirkley was oblivious to many of the tensions that could develop between the medical staff at Benanda Flying Doctor Base. Clifford, senior doctor at the Base, was aware of them all.

He stared out of the window again, frowning absently at the flat red earth which now seemed to be rising at an angle on his left as they banked sharply to head towards Broken Hill. There were two reasons for his annoyance. One was pure selfishness. He had been looking forward so much to that cool, quiet evening, and the detour to Broken Hill would delay their return considerably. Then, even when they arrived at Benanda, he could scarcely abandon the new nurse at the airstrip. She would have to be fed, delivered to her new home . . .

For a moment, Clifford wished that his sense of practicality and efficiency had not intervened to counter

Paul's proposal to pick up the girl himself. After all, it was Paul who had made all the arrangements concerning her arrival. Clifford had even forgotten that she was supposed to be coming today. Paul had outlined the arrangements, of course, but typically he had done so at a very inopportune moment, giving Clifford no chance to suggest that it might be better for her to arrive at the end of the week.

Dr Ransome's frown deepened as he thought of the junior doctor. It was difficult to understand how Paul could be so good at his job and so downright infuriating in other respects. The Base wouldn't be needing a new nurse at all if Dr Adams hadn't so thoroughly pursued Sister Gordon and then dropped her like a hot coal as soon as the poor girl had declared herself to be in love with him. Although Paul didn't even seem to be aware of the fact, Wendy Gordon had resigned purely because of their affair, and the Base had lost a good nurse.

This was the second reason for Dr Ransome's annoyance. He had no doubt at all that very much the same scenario would be enacted over the coming months with Sister Green. In large part, he blamed the girl herself. Wendy Gordon had got the job here through the proper channels, and was used to country life. But it was fairly plain to Clifford that Janet Green was rushing up here because of Paul Adams, and Paul Adams alone. It did not augur well.

Perhaps, Clifford thought ruefully, he should have refused to have her, and insisted that they look for someone closer to home as had been originally planned. He sighed.

Bill Kirkley glanced quickly sideways at the doctor when he heard the sound, but said nothing. He could easily guess the cause of his companion's annoyance, but privately thought that the chief was taking the whole thing a bit seriously. The new nurse would probably be excellent, and immune to Paul Adams' charms into the bargain.

Dr Ransome's trouble was that he needed a woman himself. A woman, Bill thought, not a pert young girl like Marcia Fairfax, who only thought she was grown up. Then he thought of the other rumour that was circulating about Dr Ransome's love-life, and shook his head. That could never be an answer either.

The two men passed the rest of the journey in easy silence, each lost in his own thoughts. Bill was the first to speak, as they approached the landing strip at Broken Hill.

'Did you feel that?'

'What? Sorry . . .' Clifford Ransome turned away from the window and looked at his pilot.

'I don't suppose you would have. There was a sort of jam and then a kick as I lowered the wheels. They're down all right now, but it might be a warning that they'll jam good and proper next time.'

'I suppose this means . . .' Clifford began.

'I'm afraid so,' Bill nodded. 'We'll have to check it. Can't take that sort of risk.'

'Of course not,' Clifford Ransome nodded.

Both men automatically accepted the stringent and vital safety standards adopted by the Royal Flying Doctor Service. When planes were landing constantly at ill-prepared and seldom-used airstrips on barren outback stations, and when they were sometimes expected to fly in dangerous conditions in order to bring an emergency case within reach of medical treatment, no chances with the mechanics of the aircraft could be taken.

This did not mean, of course, that Clifford was pleased at the prospect of delay. Quite the reverse. It seemed like just another irritation in a day that had begun well enough, but was rapidly turning sour.

'How long will it take?' he asked Bill.

'Depends what the trouble is. At least an hour, I'd say. I want to give it a thorough check.'

'That's what I thought you'd say,' Clifford said drily.

'You don't need to stay at the airport,' Bill said. 'Take Sister Green into town for a beer.'

'I will.'

A few minutes later they had taxied to a halt outside the modest terminal building. A blast of heat hit Clifford Ransome like a smack in the face when he left the aircraft. The tarmac shimmered and there was not a particle of moisture in the air. It was five o'clock, Eastern Summer Time, so the hottest part of the day was already over. He wondered grimly how the new nurse would withstand the fierce outback summer, without the cooling respite of Sydney's sparkling beaches and lush growth of shady trees that she would be used to.

Entering the terminal building was an instant relief, although even here, it was far from cool. Bill had stayed behind with the aircraft, waiting for help from a mechanic, so the doctor went into the building alone.

The East-West Airlines flight from Sydney would have landed about twenty minutes ago, so they were late and the girl should be waiting. Typically, Clifford thought, Paul would have been later still if he had been the one to collect her.

And wouldn't it be the last straw if they had gone to all this trouble and the girl wasn't on the plane?

Clifford looked across to the small lounge area. No, she was there . . .

Janet Green waited, outwardly calm and patient, but inwardly somewhat anxious and tense, in a vinyl chair by a window in the Broken Hill air terminal. She had been here for ten minutes now, and had no idea how long it would be before Paul arrived to collect her.

Two weeks ago, in Sydney, he had said that he would meet her flight in one of the Benanda Flying Doctor Base planes, but it now seemed much longer than two weeks since she had seen him, and the whole thing had taken on an air of unreality that was disconcerting for someone of her steady temperament.

She thought back carefully over how it had all happened, tracing each step as if to reassure herself that she was really here and not the victim of some kind of delusion. It had all begun at Barbara and Tracey's exam-passing celebration . . .

The party was moving rapidly into top gear. Energetic dancers, determined drinkers and animated talkers had spilled into every room now, as well as the garden, and the insistent beat of rock music on the sophisticated tape-deck provided a constant background of noise.

Janet was enjoying herself. The party was being given by two of her best friends, and she knew at least half of the guests. Many of them worked, as she did, at the South Sydney General Hospital, and many others put in regular appearances at social gatherings connected with the hospital, although they were not employed there.

Nurses Barbara Miller and Tracey Toppano were gaining a reputation for giving good parties, and Janet decided judiciously as she looked about her, that it was well-deserved. Guests had been told to 'bring a bottle or a plate', and Barbara and Tracey, with Janet's help, had been shopping and cooking all day, so there was now a generous spread of cakes, savouries, quiches, dips, cheeses and nibbles, as well as a startling variety of drinks stacked haphazardly in the kitchen. Even the bath played its part in the festivities, filled as it was with bags of crushed ice and cans of several different brands of beer.

When the first guests had arrived at half past seven, Janet had still been putting the finishing touches to her trays of savouries, and to her own outfit, which was in the required colour motif of the evening—'sterile hospital white, with touches of deathly black' Barbara and Tracey had stated with relish in their invitations.

Now it was nearly ten, and Janet actually found herself sitting down for the first time in hours, temporarily with no one to talk to. She had a drink of cool fruit punch in one hand and a piece of freshly-heated quiche in the other, and it was interesting to be able to sit back and study the party atmosphere for a while.

Most people had been both meticulous and imaginative in their dress for the party. Janet saw a girl in a stiff white ballet tutu teamed with black lace stockings, black gloves and a natty little black hat and veil perched on her black hair. A thin red-headed man, whom she recognised with a shocked laugh as one of the hospital's better-known registrars, wore full cricket whites, complete with pad, bat and gloves that had all been painted black especially for the occasion.

Only a few people—spoil-sports, Janet labelled them privately, in her usual direct way—had not accepted the strictures of the invitation. One woman was defiantly flamboyant in red and yellow, clashing horribly with everyone else, and three or four men looked as if they simply hadn't bothered, and wore their usual jeans and T-shirts.

Janet frowned absently at one of them, a stranger to her, standing with a can of beer in his hand and his elbow propped against the door jamb on the other side of the room. He would have looked nice in black and white, too, with his tall strong frame, tanned face and sun-bleached hair. Suddenly, she became disconcertingly aware that he had noticed her frowning stare, and she looked away in flushed embarrassment.

But it was too late. Their eyes had met and he had taken it as a cue to come over and speak to her, threading his way carefully through a bouncing throng of dancers and holding his beer-can high to prevent it being jostled from his hand.

'I was only invited at the last minute,' he said with an apologetic grin. 'I didn't have the right clothes. Perhaps I should have been barred at the entrance.'

'I wasn't . . .' Janet began hastily, in her surprisingly low-pitched voice.

'Yes, you were,' he interrupted, forcing her to meet

the twinkling gaze from his green eyes, and respond to his teasing smile. 'It was quite obvious. I watched you for several minutes. First you looked approvingly at several of the best-dressed guests, then you sat back and took in the general effect of the room—and I must say it is quite a striking combination of colours—then you cast scathing glances at everyone who spoiled the picture, one of whom was me.'

Janet had to laugh. He had read her face so accurately, and evidently wasn't cross.

'I'm Paul Adams,' he said. 'I'm only in Sydney for ten days, and that's my excuse for these rags.'

'Oh, they're not rags,' Janet put in quickly. He was in fact dressed very nicely in fawn cord pants and a maroon silk shirt, comfortably open around the neck as it was a warm night. 'It's simply the colours. Otherwise you look very nice.' She said it with matter-of-fact sincerity.

'Thank-you, ma'am!'

'Unlike those oafs by the kitchen door,' Janet added bluntly and unwisely. 'At least, I hope they're not friends of yours?'

'Rest assured, I don't know them from Adam, and I fully agree with you.'

They both took another look at the two men in question. Janet did not know who they were, nor who had invited them, but she could clearly see that they were very drunk, and in a loud and boorish way which she found frankly revolting.

'No, I came with Rob Treloar, over there,' Paul Adams said now, pointing to the registrar in his unusual cricketing gear. 'And I must say, when I saw his outfit I was tempted to stay home, rather than see myself so thoroughly out-classed!'

'It's all right,' Janet laughed. 'I'm sure he'll be much too uncomfortable in those pads and gloves to keep them on much longer, and then he'll look quite ordinary.'

'What's this do in aid of anyway?' Paul asked. 'Rob

didn't tell me, but it looks like something special.'

'It's special to some of us,' Janet replied. 'A celebration for passing our middies . . . midwifery course.'

'Middies!' Paul used the term with as much familiarity as Janet herself. 'Then you're a nurse, and we're in the same game. I'm a doctor.'

'Yes, I was going to ask you about that after you mentioned that you came with Dr Treloar,' Janet nodded, acknowledging to herself that she was quite pleased to have something in common with this good-looking stranger. 'You're in Sydney on holidays?'

'Sort of,' Paul nodded. 'Family obligations. My brother's getting married next Saturday and I've been roped in as best man.'

'You don't sound as though you're looking forward to it,' Janet said, her low laugh breaking out again.

'Oh, I suppose I'll enjoy it,' Paul said with exaggerated resignation. 'But it's going to be a huge affair, and I have a bachelor's horror of such things. The bride's parents are really splashing out. I'll have to be pleasant to family friends and distant relations that I haven't seen for fifteen years.'

Paul went on chatting easily to Janet for some minutes more, then suggested that he refill her glass, and returned straight away to continue their conversation. Janet was pleased that he had singled her out and was obviously so keen to stay at her side. He was an easy conversationalist—interesting, too, with his light sense of humour, and she was by no means impervious to those blond good looks as well.

Janet herself was a nice-looking young woman, and knew it without letting the fact bother her very much. She was a down-to-earth person who could make a simple and accurate assessment of her own faults and virtues and then forget about them. She was no raving beauty, she knew that, but she recognised that there were quite a few men who responded favourably to her petite, fine-boned body with its surprising reserves of strength and stamina, and to her lightly-tanned skin, grey-green eyes and frank smile.

Her friends considered her greatest asset to be her hair, and Janet herself was desperately fond of it, almost as if it were a possession that was not part of her body at all. It was straight, a rich dark blonde threaded with golden lights, and reached nearly to her knees in a heavy sweep—when she let it down, which was not often.

It was in many ways an extravagance, but it was her only one, and Janet did not begrudge the time it took to keep it washed, combed to a lustre, and trimmed. On duty at the hospital, she wore it twisted into a plain knot just above her neck, but on special occasions she experimented with loose flowing styles, or more elaborate chignons.

Tonight, for example, it was piled in glossy coils on top of her head, securely fastened with pins and decorated with tiny plaits that Barbara had painstakingly woven the day before. Half a dozen richly-scented gardenias nestled there too, and she wore three more tied with black ribbon and pinned to the simple white shirt she had chosen to team with baggy white cotton pants. Her friends had begged her to wear a dress but Janet had been adamant.

'I'm in a trouserish mood,' she had said, and defiantly added a silky black cummerbund, white tennis shoes and a man's thin black tie to the outfit.

In fact, the eccentric combination of frilly, scented flowers and masculine clothes suited her perfectly, giving her an air that was at once whimsical, precocious and careless.

Paul paid her no compliments, but she could see that he was attracted to her, and she felt happy about it, in a reckless, partyish sort of way that was unusual for her.

'It's a pity you're only here for ten days,' she said without thinking, during a brief pause in their conversation. Then she bit her lip. He would think that she was making a very obvious hint that he ask her out. She went on hastily in her low voice. 'I mean, there's so much to do in Sydney—shops, theatre, the beaches. But perhaps you're from Melbourne and have all those things there.'

She stopped, still feeling awkward. Talk about rabbiting on! It wasn't something she usually did. Tracey must have put more rum in that punch than she had thought. But Paul only smiled back quite happily as he replied,

'No, I'm not from Melbourne. And I certainly won't get time to enjoy Sydney to the full. I live in a place called Benanda, which boasts neither shops, theatres nor beaches.'

'Oh yes? Benanda . . . I don't think I've ever been there, but . . .'

'I don't expect you've even heard of it. It's way "back o'Bourke", as they say. Right in the top corner of New South Wales. And I work for the RFDS there.'

'Oh, do you really?' Janet exclaimed.

'You know what that stands for?' He was a little surprised.

'Yes. Royal Flying Doctor Service.'

The words conjured instant memories. Janet had been born in Southern Queensland after an emergency medical flight, and the Flying Doctor Service had been a part of her life for the next thirteen years on the huge outback cattle station where her family lived.

She had vivid memories of the six-monthly dental round, of the doctors' check-up flights, and of the standardised medical chest and radio transceiver with which every outback homestead was equipped.

Less pleasant memories came too—of her father's deteriorating health, of more and more radio consultations with the Flying Doctor Base, and of one frightening day when Donald Green had been carried off in the RFDS plane to Adelaide, dangerously ill, while his family had stayed behind to wait and worry.

It was ten years ago now, since the property had been sold and her family had moved to Sydney for the sake of her father's health. They had been ten happy years, full of the ordinary ups and downs of adolescence and embarking on a career, but Janet often wondered about what her life might have been like if they had stayed at Moollawindra.

'You're interested in the RFDS?' Paul was asking her now.

'Yes, I am,' Janet pulled her thoughts back to the present.

'Any particular reason?'

'Yes, actually.' She sketched the story of her early years to him and was rewarded by his quickening interest.

'Ever think of going back to the outback?'

'Yes, I do, at times,' she nodded. 'Usually on wet and windy winter days when I'm catching a bus in peak-hour traffic.'

'So you really have no serious plans to live there again?' he probed after a laugh.

Janet responded by expressing her thoughts with more consideration and gravity. Her small face fell into thoughtful lines, and she played absently with one of the tiny plaits that was working its way loose from her hair. Then she clasped her hands around her knees and stared meditatively and unseeingly at the gyrating dancers.

'I do think of going back sometimes,' she said. 'My memories of the outback are so strong. The colours, the weather, the people. I don't know if I've romanticised it. I don't think so, because I can remember horrible things, too.'

'The flies?'

'The flies,' she laughed with a nod. 'And the dust and dryness . . . and danger. It worries me sometimes that I've turned my back on it so completely, when it was such a big part of my family's history as well as my own. Moollawindra was crown land and there was nothing there before my grandfather built up the property. I don't think my younger brother and sister think about that history so much, but I do, and I could go back to the region if I wanted to. As a nurse, and especially now I'm a midwife as well, I'm sure my skills are quite in demand out "back o'Bourke".'

'They certainly are,' Paul replied, suddenly looking at her with increased speculation and interest in his eyes. 'Look, how interested are you, really, in the idea?'

'Oh!' Janet was taken aback by the change in his tone. He had leaned forward, resting his elbows against his knees, and was looking at her with frank assessment in his eyes. 'Why?' she asked him, abrupt in her turn.

'Because there's a nursing job going at my base right now. Or at least, Wendy's handed in her notice and wants to leave as soon as there's a replacement fixed up. Are you interested?'

The suddenness of the whole thing stopped Janet in her tracks for a moment. She was oblivious of the party noise still continuing around her, even though she and Paul were almost shouting to be heard above it. But she was a practical, direct girl, and one who knew her own mind.

'Yes, I am interested,' she said calmly and decidedly. 'I've only got a week's more work, then four weeks holiday. I could give in my notice straight away. I need a bit of time to relax, I think, but I could start up at Benanda in three weeks. That would be at the end of November . . .'

She was talking to herself as much as to Paul. He sat there in silence, watching the workings of her mind with friendly amusement.

'Are you making a definite offer?' she looked straight at him again to ask the question.

'To tell you the truth,' Paul replied, 'I hadn't fully thought it through myself. It was a spur of the moment suggestion. Partly as a favour to you, I suppose—and because I like you.'

This last was added with an intent that was unmistakable. 'We were planning to look more locally. That is to say, we thought someone already working in a country area would be more likely to know what's involved. But in your case . . .'

'I'm not pestering you for an answer,' Janet hastened to say.

'Of course not. We'll have to get together again to discuss it,' Paul nodded. 'In fact, perhaps we should exchange phone numbers right now.'

He grinned as he said it, and Janet felt quite certain that even if she didn't end up working with Dr Paul Adams, she would certainly see something more of him this week. She looked at his brown hands as they reached into a back pocket and pulled out a small diary. They were the capable hands of a doctor, well-kept and dappled with golden hairs. Perhaps his fingers were a little shorter, a little stubbier than those of some doctors, but they were well-shaped nonetheless, and he had probably used them to good purpose on many a woman's body before now . . .

But what a reckless turn her thoughts were taking this evening!

'Got a pencil?' Paul asked laconically.

'Tracey or Barbara will have one somewhere,' Janet said, jumping up with her usual practical energy, glad of the interruption to her musings.

Paul Adams eyed her appreciatively as she crossed the room. She would certainly be an interesting addition to Benanda society, whose attractions were dulled for Paul by thorough familiarity after a year in the small outback town. He had been out riding or picnicking with all the eligible girls, had a few good times, broken a few hearts . . .

Paul felt no qualms about those hearts. They would mend, and none of the affairs had been serious. He'd made that clear from the beginning, and assumed that the girls had taken him as lightly as he'd taken them. Wendy Gordon had been fun for a while, too, until she'd got so confounded demanding about things that life had been miserable for everyone.

The work was still fascinating though. You felt you were doing something different, and something worthwhile for other people, in that savagely beautiful region. Paul Adams, whatever else he might be, was definitely a good doctor.

But it wasn't as a doctor that he was interested in Janet Green, with her unusual looks and straight-forward personality. She was going to be a bit different from most of the women he had known . . .

She came towards him again now, the curves of her compact figure tantalisingly concealed beneath the loose shirt and trousers. Many women would have looked disastrous dressed as she was, but Janet could carry it off. Perhaps it was that hair. Paul could well appreciate its gloss and thickness, but could only guess at its length. Over the coming week, however, he intended to find out, if he could, exactly how long it was—and how it felt between his fingers.

'Let's dance!'

He pulled her to her feet after phone numbers had been exchanged, and they joined the press of bodies still energetically throwing themselves about in the centre of the room. Two hours later, when Rob Treloar was ready to leave, Janet was not in the least surprised that Paul should try to kiss her.

'Walk me to the gate?' he said softly to her, as Dr Treloar went ahead to wait in the car.

'Okay,' Janet replied, softly as well.

When they reached the small iron gate, overhung by a luxuriously mauve-blossomed jacaranda tree, she felt his warm arm against her shoulders, gently stopping her, and she turned to him without reluctance.

''Night,' he said against her cheek, then folded his arms around her and found her lips.

She responded. It was a very nice kiss. In the past few years, Janet had experienced a healthy number of them, as well as things that went a bit further, and Paul's mouth was smooth and expert. But she was aware that other people were beginning to leave now, and their position was a little too public for her taste.

'It's been lovely,' she said to him as she pulled gently but firmly away. He accepted the signal and stepped back, jaunty once more.

'I'll ring you about the job on Monday, as soon as I've contacted the Base and got a second opinion.'

'Good!' Janet turned and walked back up the front steps and into the house, a little chilly in the night air now that the warmth of his arms was gone. She did not look back. She wasn't a girl who mooned after a man she had known only for one evening.

Paul was as good as his word and rang Janet's flat at eleven on Monday morning. She had stayed till the end of Saturday's party, in order to help Barbara and Tracey with the clearing up, and had worked a B shift on Sunday from three till eleven. This had left her tired, so she was still lazing over a late breakfast when the phone sounded.

'Changed your mind since Saturday?' were Paul's careless first words after they had exchanged a greeting.

Janet hadn't. In fact, the idea had taken root in her mind and had seemed more exciting the more she thought about it. Many of the nurses in the midwifery course were not staying on at the South Sydney General. Some were transferring to other hospitals, some were taking off on long-planned trips overseas, and one or two were actually having babies themselves. Janet's flatmate was moving to Brisbane with her boyfriend. Change was in the late spring air, and Janet's spirit was affected by it.

'No, I haven't changed my mind,' she said to Paul. 'What's the story?'

'You can have the job.'

'Really? As simple as that?' Janet's normally deep voice rose in a squeak of excitement that she could not suppress.

It would be a completely new life, and a challenging one, but she was suddenly more than ready for it. It was time she did something like this. It would be easy to give up the flat. Everything pointed to the new job being right.

'Really as simple as that,' Paul laughed back at her down the phone. 'I've spoken to South Sydney about your qualifications, and I've checked with Base at Benanda. End of the month suit you?'

'I . . . I think so.' She remembered that she had said three weeks the other night, but had nevertheless been expecting that she would have a bit longer to prepare. Things were moving very fast.

'What about meeting over dinner tonight to discuss it further, finalise the details and so forth?' His tone had become more intimate.

'Oh, I can't, I'm sorry,' Janet said with real regret. 'I have to work. Only four more shifts, but they're all three till eleven.'

For a moment Paul sounded disappointed and a little irritated at the spoiling of his plan, but then he suggested lunch the following day, and they ate it at a harbour-side restaurant, lingering until she was nearly late for work.

Then on Friday she *was* free, and he took her to the beach then dinner and kissed her again, and she decided that living in the same small town with him might be very nice.

He had ended the evening by saying lightly but meaningfully, 'I'll see you in two and a half weeks at Benanda,' so she was surprised to hear his voice on the phone again on Saturday morning.

'Do you want to come to my brother's wedding?'

'That would be lovely . . . but at such short notice?'

'I know. Doesn't matter if you can't make it,' he said. 'It's just that the cousin I was going to escort has gone down with glandular fever and can't make it. I thought straight away of you.'

'I'll spend the rest of the day worrying about what to wear,' Janet joked after she had accepted the surprise offer.

'Wear anything,' Paul replied. 'As long as I get a glimpse of that hair out loose.'

'Oh, I couldn't,' Janet said immediately. 'I'd be far too hot.'

They had been having an early taste of summer all that week, and again today the air was uncomfortably warm.

'You'll have to get used to the heat if you're going to like Benanda,' was Paul's rejoinder.

They finalised arrangements for the afternoon, and then he rang off after being called away by an obviously harassed parent in the background. His comment about the heat had started a worry in Janet's mind, however. Her hair might be a problem in a hotter climate. The fact had not occurred to her before, but now she started to think about it.

Its hot weight on top of her head, and clinging damply to her in its night-time braids—how easy would it be to keep it clean in a dry and dusty environment where water was scarce?

'I *couldn't* cut it!' she thought. 'I'll manage it somehow. It'll be under a cap at work, I suppose. Perhaps if I have a few inches trimmed off before I go up there . . .'

After this decision, she refused to go on worrying about it, but occasionally it did nag at the back of her mind . . .

As Paul had indicated, the wedding was a splendid affair, and Janet could only be glad that she was able to take a background role, feeling nice and anonymous in her simple dress of forest green patterned voile. The ceremony itself, in one of Sydney's biggest Catholic churches, took over an hour, and the reception, held in the grounds of one of Sydney's historic old houses, which was now a function centre, seemed crowded and lively.

Janet was aware of interest and speculation directed at

her from both sides of the newly-weds' families. She was introduced to the bride and groom, and both sets of parents. Susan Adams' father asked with a chuckle if Janet was hoping to catch the bride's bouquet later on when the couple left, and added, 'Perhaps we can expect you to snaffle up young Paul. What about it, eh?'

'I can hardly say at this stage,' Janet replied. 'I've only known him for a week.'

She always hated to be rushed into a relationship, especially by outsiders, and didn't like to have romantic developments in her life scrutinised publicly either. Privacy was something Janet valued a lot.

But it was the new bride who provided the most disturbing comments of the evening. She was chatting to Janet towards the end of the reception, and they both noticed Paul a dozen yards away, an arm around two girls at once.

'Well, Paul's certainly getting his usual share of the talent!' Susan Adams commented.

'You don't approve?' Janet ventured.

'Oh, no! It's not that. I'm very fond of my new brother-in-law. But he's an outrageous flirt. I'm sure you don't need me to tell you that,' Susan said. 'Although I gather you haven't known him long. A lot of men talk about marriage being a trap, but most of them don't mean it. Paul does though. I can't imagine him ever settling down.'

'You can't?'

'No. He'll move back to the city in a year or two, start acquiring possessions. A boat probably, and a nice apartment. But in ten years or so, he'll start to get lonely and he won't know what to do about it. I have an older cousin who's exactly the same.'

At that moment, Susan was approached for a kiss by an old friend who had to leave early. This gave Janet the chance to observe the bride quite closely, and she was glad of it. The new Mrs Adams was not at all pretty, but she had a face that was both compassionate and intelligent, and Janet instinctively trusted her insight into Paul's character and future.

A faint pang of disappointment weighed inside Janet for a moment, because she did find Paul an attractive and fun-filled companion, but she shook it off. It would be stupid to be hurt after knowing him for such a short time, just as it would be stupid to think that she could change a happy bachelor into a family man.

'We'll still be friends, but I just won't get in too deep,' Janet decided.

Susan's comment had been a lucky one, helping her to be aware of the danger of thinking too much about Paul's part in her new life. It wasn't because of Paul that she had decided to go to Benanda, and it was important to remember that.

He was leaving for Benanda tomorrow, in any case, and two weeks later, Janet herself would be taking the same route north-west. Meanwhile, she had a million things to do—her flat to clear out, decisions to make about what to take and what to leave, and a long round of farewells to family and friends.

Janet knew that, whatever happened at Benanda, she was now at the start of a new phase in her life, and she would not be able to remain unchanged by it.

CHAPTER TWO

JANET was more certain of this than ever as she sat quietly waiting in her chair at the airport. It was twenty minutes since her arrival and still Paul had not turned up, but no doubt he would do so soon.

A light plane had landed a few minutes ago, and she had waited eagerly for the sight of his strong silhouette and blond head, but the man who stepped from the plane had been taller, slimmer, and quite dark.

Janet had already told the airline clerk who she was and who should be collecting her. Perhaps in a while she would have to return to his desk and ask him if it was possible to ring Benanda Base to find out what had happened.

Just then, the dark man from the plane entered the building, sending a blast of hot air through the already tepid atmosphere as he opened the door. Janet had only a few moments to wonder who he was—a local property owner? a visiting business man? a mining engineer? —before she realised that he was coming to speak to her. It must be one of the pilots from the Base, then, sent to collect her instead of Paul.

He looked stern and stiff, and Janet could not help a wave of disappointment washing over her. She was quite tired and a long way from home, and it would have been nice to feel Paul's welcoming arms. Stupidly, as the pilot arrived at her seat, she blurted out a betrayal of her feelings.

'Where's Paul?'

The man frowned and stiffened even further.

'It didn't make sense for Paul to collect you when my plane was in the area,' he said crisply, then held out a brown hand. 'I'm Dr Ransome, Clifford Ransome. And of course you are Janet Green.'

'Yes, yes I am.' Janet pulled herself together.

It had been silly to greet a stranger with such an obvious hint that she wanted him to be someone else, and this was the senior doctor at the Base, not a pilot, who might have been more easy-going about her lapse.

'It's very nice to meet you,' she made herself add brightly.

'Yes, nice to meet you, too. I'm sure we'll enjoy working together,' Dr Ransome said smoothly, in a way that gave Janet the distinct impression that he wasn't sure of this at all. He eyed her suitcase and sports carry-bag. 'Is this all you've brought?'

'Yes.'

She couldn't tell from his tone if he approved or not. His broad yet fine-boned shoulders were set very square beneath his short-sleeved white cotton shirt, and the frown had not relaxed from his features once.

'We'll put your things in the plane now,' he was saying. 'But I'm afraid we can't take off for a while. Mechanical problems. Nothing serious, we hope, but it'll be at least an hour. I'll take you into town for a cool drink.'

'There's no need.' Janet responded quickly to the sheer weariness in his tone. He had obviously had a long day.

'*I* need one,' he replied tersely, 'even if you don't. And I'd rather have a drive than sit here twiddling my thumbs for an hour.'

He cast a scathing glance around the terminal building, which Janet felt was a little unfair. It wasn't so bad! The doctor stepped past her to pick up her suitcase, and she bent quickly down to take the carry-bag, then followed him out onto the tarmac to the little plane.

It was different from the ones she remembered from her childhood. More modern, of course. A Piper Chieftain, Paul had said, which could be equipped with oxygen, resuscitation units, humidicribs and various other examples of modern medical equipment.

Dr Ransome took her carry-bag and loaded it into the plane while Janet stood by, getting only a glimpse of the neat interior. A hot breeze blew across the tarmac, and she welcomed the small amount of shade and shelter provided by the plane. She noticed two men approaching from a nearby hangar, one neatly dressed, and the other clad in blue mechanic's overalls. Dr Ransome had not gone into much detail about the 'mechanical problems' and she wondered about them. What if it took longer than an hour to fix?

'How about that drink now?' Clifford said to the new nurse as he emerged from the plane.

He was attempting to be a little more cheerful and friendly, although his misgivings about the girl were not diminishing. She was probably nice enough in her way, but she belonged in a city with that diminutive build and fine, eager features, and he could not trust or respect someone who would come all the way out here because of a light affair with a good-looking young doctor. The outback had broken stronger spines and tested deeper attachments than those of Janet Green, Clifford Ransome knew that only too painfully well.

She nodded, relieved, at his mention of the drink. She was obviously hot and thirsty. Clifford noticed a small yet firm hand reach to the collar of her apricot cotton blouse and loosen it further, then move higher to the thick pile of hair on top of her head, to reposition a pin.

'Let's get moving then,' he said, and stepped from the shade of the aircraft.

Janet followed suit, just as a stronger gust of wind buffeted across the tarmac. It caught at her light-weight cream linen skirt and flapped it up and then across against her thighs, revealing their outlines clearly, and showing them to be slightly sturdier than Clifford had expected.

She might be small, but she wasn't anorexic, and she

had a good deal of healthy muscle. He was about to ask
her what sports she played, but then the wind gusted
again, and this time it caught her hair and it came
tumbling down her back, the golden lights shining in
the late afternoon sun. It cascaded to an incredible
length.

Clifford gasped unwittingly. It was an incredibly
beautiful sight. But Janet was already bending down,
searching desperately for the pins she had lost, holding
the rope of hair away from the oil splodges that covered
the ground, with one hand, and collecting pins with the
other.

Clifford bent down beside her to help, and caught the
faint balsam scent that must come from the shampoo she
used. He found three pins and returned them gravely to
her, saw her faint flush and nod of thanks, then watched
as she picked up her bag and began to walk ahead of him
into the terminal building, already winding her hair into
a knot as she went.

For a moment, he knew a mad impulse to call after
her: 'Leave it out, it's so lovely.' Then he was angry with
himself, and with her.

How on earth did she think she'd get on in this
environment and climate with that Rapunzel-like rope?
It would have to go, and he would tell her so straight
away—before that image of its shining fall gets too
indelibly printed in your brain, the small voice of con-
science told him.

Janet was embarrassed by the whole incident, and
steeled herself for the inevitable comments and questions which she always hated, in spite of her fondness for
her heavy tresses. If the wind was often like that, she
would have to fasten it even more securely than she did
in Sydney. Hopping in and out of planes on windy
landing strips would test her skill in that area every
day.

She kept up her quickened pace so that she would
arrive at the shelter of the terminal before the doctor and

have time to fasten the last pins carefully. But he was walking more rapidly now, too, and with his long strides, he soon caught up to her.

'You'll have to chop off that hair.'

The blunt words came from just behind Janet, taking her breath with their suddenness. She was immediately on the defensive, and angry too, because Dr Ransome had voiced her own nagging fear. She turned to face him as he held open the door for her.

'I won't,' she said. 'I'll manage it.'

'Out here? On duty?'

'It'll be under my cap,' she countered. It was scarcely the way she usually talked to someone she had just met, but Dr Ransome seemed to be in a bad mood that was contagious.

'Our nurses don't wear caps,' was his retort.

'Then . . . then, I'll wear a scarf—a white one—if that's all right,' Janet improvised rapidly.

'What's the point of having such lovely hair if no one sees it?' Clifford asked now, more gently, but Janet was not in the mood to be conciliatory.

'I'll decide for myself.'

She spoke the words with an unmistakable finality, disliking Clifford Ransome more every minute, and feeling more sorry than ever that Paul had not been the one to meet her. During their times together in Sydney, he had offered nothing but praise for her 'crowning glory', as he teasingly called it, and had never once suggested that it might not be practical.

Janet waited while Dr Ransome spoke to the airline clerk, asking if he could borrow the man's car for the trip into town. Obviously they knew each other reasonably well, as the car keys were handed over without hesitation. The clerk tipped a wink to Janet then went back to his paper work, and Clifford led the way to the small car park outside the front of the building.

'If we had more time, I could show you over the Broken Hill RFDS Base,' Dr Ransome said as they climbed into the vehicle, a compact four-wheel drive, well-suited to the region's bumpy roads, and equipped Janet noticed happily, with air-conditioning. 'It's bigger than ours, and has a School of the Air section, which we don't. We only started up a couple of years ago to take some of the load off Broken Hill and Charlesville and Mount Isa, so Broken Hill has more links than we have with the whole history of the Service.'

'Yes, it would have been interesting to see it,' Janet nodded sincerely.

'We can do that and skip the drink if you'd like . . .' He suppressed a weary sigh.

'No, let's not. There'll be other times won't there?' Janet said quickly. 'I'm thirsty.'

She was, increasingly so, but knew that he felt the need of liquid refreshment even more than she did after his long day. Studying him covertly as they drove, Janet saw that his tanned face showed traces of dust, and sweat glistened at his throat and on his temple, although the air-conditioner was rapidly taking effect in the small cabin of the vehicle.

It was difficult to guess at his age. Around thirty, Janet hazarded, although his dark eyes were narrowed against the glare of the road ahead, emphasising the fine wrinkles around them.

Clifford slowed outside a pub in the main street of the town, then sped up again. A crowd of men enjoying a drink after a long day's work had spilled out onto the verandah, and he knew that the atmosphere of the place would be raucous and a little brutish. A quiet café and a long icy chocolate milkshake was more what he felt like, and he guessed that Janet would feel the same.

The milk-bar he chose was quite a pleasant place—of the laminex table-top variety, but, he reflected, if Janet Green expected to find the kind of trendy little café that abounded in Sydney where an iced chocolate cost more than two dollars and the waiters had pink hair, she was destined for disappointment.

In fact, the new nurse showed no noticeable reaction to the décor, and they sat in silence until after the waitress had served the milkshakes. Clifford himself felt no inclination to speak, but decided in the end that he should. After all, he had to establish some reasonable kind of relationship with the girl since they were to be working together—even if it was only a couple of months before she fled back to the city, nursing heat exhaustion and a heart severely bruised by Paul Adams!

Clifford had already decided that he would keep Sister Green away from the junior doctor as much as possible during working hours, putting Paul onto flights where a nurse was not required, but they were bound to see a lot of each other off duty, and that's where the damage would be done.

'Do you have any questions about the work?' He had made the query sound like one asked at a job interview, but felt too tired to think of small talk which would put her at ease. He wasn't a talkative type. Besides, the sceptical part of him wanted to get some idea of what expectations she had about life at Benanda. It was the part of him which was maliciously pleased to note that she seemed flustered by his question.

'Oh . . . er . . . let me think,' Janet said, bumped out of a weary reverie by his words. She had been quite content with the silence between them, and always hated any situation in which she felt obliged to chatter. 'Questions . . . I read as much as I could about the Service before I came up . . .'

She did not mention her own past links with it and the region, presuming that Paul would have mentioned them to his superior.

'Yes, there are several books, aren't there?' Clifford nodded. 'Mostly written for the layman.'

Janet read a criticism of herself in his last words.

'It's difficult to get hold of anything else,' she said. 'The RFDS Section headquarters in Sydney gave me some pamphlets when I was filling in various forms there. They were actually very helpful, but you can never really know what a job is going to entail until you start doing it.'

'That's true,' Dr Ransome conceded.

Janet bent over her straw for a moment, then glanced up at him. His face was impassive. It was an interesting face, she decided. Very attractive, with that quirky, boyish smile and intelligent forehead . . .

Janet told herself that she was making these observations quite dispassionately. She had already made up her mind that it was going to be difficult to like Clifford Ransome, and she would much rather have been sitting here with Paul. Deep brown eyes that held a touch of enigmatic sadness, and thick dark hair that fell in slight waves against his well-shaped head were not enough to compensate for defects of personality.

'Finished your drink? We should be getting back.' He cut across her thoughts with the words.

'A few more mouthfuls,' Janet said, and sucked them up hastily. She could feel the table vibrating slightly as he tapped an impatient foot unconsciously. He stifled a yawn, too.

'He seems to like me about as much as I like him,' Janet thought. 'I hope that's not going to make things difficult.'

It shouldn't. Janet had worked with people she disliked before, and was too sensible to tie herself up in angry knots over their behaviour. Oh, she had a bit of a temper, but could usually talk herself out of it pretty quickly, or work it off on a tennis court or jogging path.

During the drive back out to the airfield, Dr Ransome roused himself to be more communicative, telling her a few things about the history of the town and pointing out a few groups of kangaroos who were beginning to emerge for their evening feeding session from the patches of shade where they had rested during the day.

'Plane's ready, Bill says,' the clerk informed them laconically when they arrived back.

'What was the trouble, did he say?' Clifford Ransome asked.

'Mashed grasshoppers in the works,' the clerk grinned. Janet shuddered slightly at the too-graphic description.

'That's right. We did hit a few clouds of them,' Clifford nodded.

'But they checked over the other possibilities, just in case,' the clerk added.

'So we can leave straight away?' The doctor was clearly itching to do so.

'Fifteen minutes. We're waiting on a landing—plane from up Innamincka way. Something to do with the film they're making up there.'

The clerk was clearly prepared to make conversation, but Dr Ransome only sighed between clenched teeth and frowned down at his watch. Janet glanced at an electric clock on the wall. Twenty to seven already. That meant darkness would be coming on by the time they arrived at Benanda. Presumably the airstrip there had some kind of landing lights, but it meant she would not get much of a view of the town as they came in to land, which was a pity.

Dr Ransome summoned up some acceptably polite thanks for the use of the clerk's car, and Janet wondered if he always found it so difficult to be courteous. But the man behind the counter looked suddenly sympathetic.

'Late night, Doc?'

'Two hours' sleep,' Clifford Ransome replied. 'We had an emergency night flight. And the night before wasn't much better. I can't wait to get home.'

Janet bit her lip and felt a little guilty about her own uncharitable thoughts. As a nurse, she should have been at least as perceptive as the air terminal clerk and seen that Clifford Ransome's weariness was deeper than just that caused by a hot day's work.

'Could I get you some coffee from somewhere?' she blurted out, frowning at him in her concern. He met her gaze.

'Thanks, but it would only keep me awake later on when I'm ready for bed.'

He moved to a chair, picked up a current affairs weekly from the small magazine table in front of him and began to flip through its pages. Janet sat down too, took a paperback from her bag and began to read. But it wasn't a particularly good book, and she couldn't keep her concentration. She was aware, for no good reason, of every tired movement made by the tall, economically-built man opposite her.

His weariness was infectious, and the terminal building was stuffy. Janet stifled a yawn . . .

'Innamincka plane's down,' the clerk said ten endless minutes later. Janet rose to her feet with an effort.

'You look almost as bad as I feel,' Clifford Ransome said, and then suddenly, surprisingly, they were both laughing.

'And you look as though you *feel* about ninety years old. Oh dear!' Janet returned.

'See you two around,' the clerk said, also more cheerfully, as they left the building.

The tarmac still felt like an oven, and though the wind had dropped a bit, Janet put a hand up to her hair instinctively to push in two loose pins. She glanced almost fearfully at Clifford Ransome as she caught herself in this action, but he was striding ahead with desperate energy, as if he just couldn't wait to be on the plane.

It was just after eight when they cruised in to a gentle landing at Benanda Flying Doctor Base airstrip. The sky was still full of red and gold and mauve, and after all, Janet could get quite a good idea of the layout of the small town. In a part of the country where land was not at a premium, Benanda's streets were wider than most of Sydney's, although they carried only a fraction of the traffic. Narrow strips of bitumen bordered by broad expanses of red earth ran down the main street and a few side streets, and most of the houses were small places with screened-in verandahs and weatherboard walls.

Some were raised on pillars to allow air—and sometimes flood-waters—to circulate beneath. Janet remembered such places from outback towns in Queensland that she had visited as a child, and suddenly the desert settlement did not seem so very unfamiliar.

Her legs were stiff as she climbed from the plane, having passed her luggage down to Bill Kirkley before she did so. Dr Ransome was the last to leave the plane, and once on the ground he wasted no time.

'Bill, I'll see you in the morning. Janet, we'll walk to my place. It's quite near. And I'll phone Lorna to say you've arrived and find out what's going on.'

'Lorna?'

'Mrs Hammond. You're boarding with her. I hope the arrangement will suit you. It'll have to, actually, because there is no other accommodation in the town, unless you fancy residing permanently at the Drover's Dream Hotel, which I certainly wouldn't.'

He was walking—quite rapidly—as he spoke, and Janet followed him, carry-bag in hand.

'Is Mrs Hammond's where the girl before me . . . Wendy?—is that where she stayed?' Janet asked.

'Yes, and Petra, who was our first, before that.'

'Then I'm sure it will be all right.'

'Good.'

They were passing a sprawling wide-verandahed building which Janet assumed must be the Base itself, then through a gate and into a large back-yard, which was only boundaried on this one side.

'This is my place,' Clifford flung back at her as he climbed five wooden steps at the back of the house, opened a screen door, crossed the enclosed verandah, took a key from under the mat and opened the door.

'Shut that screen door quickly, would you? Or we'll be invaded by mozzies and flying ants.'

Janet obeyed quickly and sent a blessing to her mother who had reminded her to pack insect repellent. Dr Ransome put down Janet's suitcase, switched on a light, then motioned his new nurse inside.

'Have a glass of water and sit down,' he said. 'Or if you need to use the bathroom, go through that door and down the passage. It's at the end. I'll ring up Lorna in a minute, but if you'll excuse me, the first thing I'm going to do is wash my feet—and I'd advise you to keep your distance, because my socks will probably stand up by themselves!'

He gave a tired, twisted, but cheerful grin, but before Janet could decide how to respond, he had gone out of the back door again, and she heard him begin to run cold water into a plastic bucket in the laundry.

Left to herself, Janet was not quite sure which of his suggestions to take up first, so she stood awkwardly in the kitchen for a moment or two, then began half-heartedly to look for a glass for water as she listened to the satisfied splashings and squelchings that came from outside.

Clifford returned just as she was rinsing out the glass she had found. He was bare-footed, stretching clean brown toes luxuriously as he walked and looking distinctly more energetic if not more friendly.

'Just sit on the verandah while I ring Lorna,' he said. 'I'll get you a drink in a minute, and there should be some papers out there. I imagine you're probably too late for dinner at Lorna's, but we'll knock up something here.'

He opened a side door and ushered her on to a section of the verandah that was wider than the back part. Then he flicked a light switch and returned inside, leaving Janet to choose one of the three floral-patterned armchairs.

She was surprised and impressed at what she had seen

of the doctor's house. He obviously lived here alone —she had seen no evidence of a second person during her brief visit to the bathroom. One toothbrush, one towel . . . And he must be a very busy man, yet the house was as well-kept as it would have been by a full-time housewife. Quiet good taste showed everywhere, too, and it was clear that Clifford Ransome liked his house to be a tranquil and pleasant retreat from the harsh climate and from the demands of his job.

This verandah, for example. The wooden floor boards were stained a smooth dark brown, and the varnish on top was shining and new. Cool to the touch, too, Janet found after she had followed the doctor's example and slipped off her sandals.

Outside, the retreating glow of the sunset revealed oleander, bougainvillaea, acacias and other colourful shrubs that pressed up against the house and two rain-water tanks, adding greenness and life. Inside the screened-off space, pot plants of all shapes and sizes abounded, arranged in groups on the floor, in tiered stands, and in hanging baskets of cane or woven sea-grass.

There was even a large fish tank containing two goldfish. It was set safely against the wall out of reach of the sun, and this presence of water added to the cool feeling of the outdoor room. A wide shelf of books was also set against the wall, and above it was a series of Japanese prints, featuring delicate water-colour impressions of mountains, temperate forest greenery, and animal life.

Janet had only just finished examining all this when the doctor returned.

'I was right about your dinner,' he said. 'She had made you some, but you were later than she expected so she's sold it.'

'*Sold* it?'

'Yes, to a passing truck-driver. She runs the local petrol station and road-house.'

'Oh.'

'She doesn't normally do hot dinners, just pies and sandwiches and so forth, but she said he was so hungry, and she didn't want the food to go to waste if you weren't coming till tomorrow . . . so you will have to eat here.'

Janet had been about to laugh at the way he was imitating what must be Lorna Hammond's gossipy way of speaking, but after his last words, he tossed her a quick, harried look that communicated his weariness once again.

'What about the hotel?' she said hastily. 'Wouldn't they do counter teas?'

'From half past six to half past seven, and it's now eight-thirty. This isn't the city, you know.'

'Yes, I *do* know,' Janet retorted sharply, her temper flaring at his short manner and deliberate criticism. 'I'm just trying to save you trouble. I can see that you're exhausted and would much rather be alone. I'll go without dinner, if you like—or I'm sure Mrs Hammond would let me buy a pie . . .'

'Well, I'm starving, so since I'm cooking for myself, you might as well share it,' Clifford Ransome said.

'I'll help you cook.'

'Don't . . . Please.' He found a smile, but was obviously controlling weariness and irritation with difficulty. 'I mean it. You don't know where anything is. I like my kitchen. It's organised how I want it, and . . .'

'I understand,' Janet said quickly, feeling a sudden wash of sympathy for him. He really must be exhausted.

As he turned away to return to the kitchen, she felt an absurd impulse to go to him and pull his head down towards her in order to massage away the tension from his face and shoulders with firm, gentle fingers—but she resisted it, of course.

Five minutes later he was back, carrying two brandy-and-drys and a plate of biscuits and cheese on a tray.

'You don't mind waiting for the meal, do you?' he said. 'I'd like to sit down with this drink for ten minutes.

The biscuits will keep the wolf from the door, and I told Lorna you'd be a while.'

'That's fine,' Janet assured him, accepting the cold-misted glass he held out, and listening with relief to the clink of the ice.

The day's heat was seeping quickly out of the earth, but it was still very warm. Clifford moved another armchair close to her own and put the tray on a small coffee table in between, within easy reach of both of them.

Neither spoke as they ate and drank, but the silence was quite companionable, interrupted as it was by only the sounds of the night, of Clifford's newspaper rustling, the crack of biscuits, and the crunch and tinkle of ice. Crickets rasped out their strident tune, moths beat themselves against the fine wire mesh in their frantic attempts to reach the light, and in the distance a generator—or perhaps it was a water-pump?—throbbed rhythmically.

At the top-most range of her hearing, Janet could detect the squeak of bats, too, as they flitted through the night in search of insects.

There was something very soothing about all these bush sounds. Janet's limbs relaxed, and she felt strangely content to be sitting on the verandah of the doctor's pleasant house.

'This place needs a woman,' she found herself thinking. 'A wife. It's so nice. A woman would appreciate it.'

Still, after that comment Dr Ransome had made about his kitchen . . . It seemed that he had no desire to let another person near it. Janet appreciated organisation and efficiency herself, but she had managed to share kitchens with disorganised people in the past. It seemed that Clifford Ransome wasn't so tolerant. Perhaps both the doctors at Benanda Flying Doctor Base would turn out to be confirmed bachelors.

Gradually her thoughts became easier and lighter,

and she scarcely noticed when Dr Ransome rose to go
and prepare the meal. By the time it was ready, she had
fallen asleep in her chair, and it was only the knock of the
wooden tray on the surface of the coffee table which
woke her.

'Mind if we eat off our laps?' Dr Ransome said, when
he returned with a second tray.

'Not at all,' Janet replied, stretching her muscles and
sitting up straight in her chair. The meal was a simple,
homey one, but it looked appetising.

'I can't eat all that!' she exclaimed as she took in the
fried egg on toast, crisp bacon, sausages, onion, grilled
tomatoes and baked beans. There was a simple side-
salad of tossed lettuce, too, flavoured with tangy Italian
dressing. Freshly squeezed orange juice in a tall glass
completed the meal.

'You'll need it,' Clifford Ransome said. 'I'm afraid
you've got a hard day tomorrow. We're off on the
second leg of our regular clinic flight, and we'll be
staying out over-night.'

'Staying out?' Janet had sudden visions of a desert
encampment of tents beside the Piper Chieftain, set
down in the middle of nowhere.

'Yes, they'll put us up at Glencoe Downs. It's about
350 miles from here,' Clifford explained, chasing away
Janet's slightly alarming fantasy.

'Oh, right,' she nodded, not entirely relieved.

The doctor tossed a narrow glance at her.

'Sorry to spring it on you,' he said. 'But we can't
change our routine just because you've chosen to arrive
today.'

It was difficult not to read criticism of herself into his
tone.

'But I thought . . . At least, it was Paul who suggested
what day I should arrive,' Janet said, truthfully but
defensively.

'Yes, I suppose it was,' Dr Ransome returned smoothly. 'He didn't think. You'll have to take the matter up

with him if you're annoyed about it, but the fact remains that we need a nurse for the rest of the clinic flight. It was damned inconvenient trying to manage without one today. Wendy left last weekend, and the temporary nurse from Broken Hill had to go back sooner than expected, for some reason. The whole thing has been a mess ever since Sister Gordon handed in her notice.'

'Well, I can't see that that's my fault,' Janet retorted coolly. 'But if you'll tell me exactly what I should bring for tomorrow, and what time to meet you and where, then naturally I'll be prepared.'

'Oh, I'll pick you up from Lorna's,' Dr Ransome sighed, as if this petty detail was simply the last straw. 'At a quarter past seven. I'll bring a uniform for you. Apart from that, whatever you'd normally bring for a night away from home.'

After this, they finished the meal in silence, while Janet digested all the new information he had offered. It was an unsettling start to her new life—arriving at Mrs Hammond's so late tonight, then setting off so early again tomorrow, *and* spending the night away from her new home. She felt a sudden spurt of annoyance against Paul, with his too-casual ways. He must have known that the clinic flight was taking place—clearly it was a regular and pre-planned event—yet he had said nothing about it and blithely told her to book herself on the Monday afternoon plane.

Paul . . . Janet wondered when she would see him. Not tonight, that was certain.

'Will Paul be on the clinic flight tomorrow?'

Clifford paused in the act of piling up the dirty crockery, then looked at Janet directly and coolly.

'No, he won't.'

He offered no further explanation, but went into the kitchen to leave the dishes on the sink, then picked up both Janet's bags and went out the back door without speaking. Janet took this as a signal that she was to follow and skipped hastily after him, round to the other side of the house where a small four-wheel-drive vehicle stood waiting.

Infuriatingly, her hair had again slipped down as she bumped down the back steps. She would have to plait it each day before coiling it around her head.

Dr Ransome stowed her bags in the back of the vehicle, then came round to the passenger door to unlock it for Janet.

'No one else in Benanda locks their car,' he said. 'But I happen to have a medicine chest in mine, so I take precautions.'

'Yes, you can't presume that drug abuse is confined to the cities, can you?' Janet nodded, venturing a slight smile at him. She had decided to pretend not to care about her hair.

The doctor had not moved after unlocking the door, but still stood there and she could see he was looking at her.

'Your hair's come down again.' The words were spoken quite softly.

'I know.'

'It's lovely.' He reached out a warm hand and twisted a thick strand of it softly between his fingers, then let it fall.

Janet felt a sudden spark of sexual awareness flare within her, and knew that he felt it too. For a tiny moment, it even seemed possible that he would kiss her, but before she could know whether he wanted to or not, she stepped back. Their eyes still held each other's gaze, however.

'I thought you said I had to have it cut off,' she challenged him softly, not knowing why she was reminding him of his earlier words.

'You do.'

He cocked his head slightly to one side and gave a half-smile as he spoke, then moved nimbly towards the front of the vehicle and climbed into the driver's seat.

Janet was disturbed by what had happened—by its

unexpectedness more than anything else, perhaps. Paul Adams had been openly interested in her as a woman from the first, but Clifford Ransome had clearly thought of her mainly as an irritating circumstance interfering with the well-run routine of his life, and somehow that felt a lot safer to Janet.

The small moment at the door of the car—how long had it lasted? Only a few seconds, surely! Even though it was now past, it had added a complexity to their wary feelings about each other which she did not want at all.

But the best thing to do was to forget about it and tell herself that it wouldn't be likely to happen again.

The journey by vehicle to Mrs Hammond's roadhouse at the far side of town took only a few minutes, but Janet calculated that it would be at least fifteen minutes on foot. She wondered, practical as ever, how she would get to the Flying Doctor Base quickly enough in an emergency, but felt too tired to ponder the question seriously.

The petrol station with its adjoining shop was in darkness, but as the sound of the car engine died, a light came on outside some rooms at the end of the building, and in a moment a plump figure in a floral dress had appeared at the screen door.

'Here at long last, Lorna!' Dr Ransome called.

'Don't worry,' Mrs Hammond said cheerfully. 'I won't be ready for bed for another hour, but I guess this young lady is pretty tired.'

She came to meet Janet and patted her on the arm in a friendly way.

'I've just put the kettle on,' she said. 'Like a cuppa?'

'Yes, that would be very nice,' Janet said, not truthfully. She would rather have been shown her room and been able to go straight to bed, but sensed that her new landlady would be curious about her, and she felt obliged to share a hot drink and a short chat. She glanced briefly at Clifford Ransome and saw his short approving nod, so she knew she had done the right thing.

To Janet's surprise, Mrs Hammond did not lead the way indoors, but went around the side of the building instead.

'Ron and I were going to put a motel out the back here six years ago,' she said. 'The year before he died, it was. At that stage there was talk that the road to the new gasfields would go through Benanda and link up with the MacDonald Highway up north. There would have been a good trade with that. We got as far as building the caretaker's unit and pegging out the rest, then we found they'd changed their minds and were putting the road out west, across from South Australia. We lost a bit of money through that, but now it comes in very handy for the nurses.'

She opened the door of the small besser-brick dwelling. It was neatly if cheaply furnished, and had two small rooms as well as an adequate bathroom.

The combined lounge and kitchen contained a tiny fridge, an electric stove and a radio, as well as a table and several chairs, both straight-backed and easy. There was a rickety bookshelf, too, containing an assortment of paperbacks which Janet promised herself she would examine when she got back from the clinic flight on Wednesday.

'Petra and Wendy both had the same arrangement,' Lorna Hammond was explaining. 'Breakfast and lunch and snacks they fixed for themselves in here, and I did dinner for them in my own kitchen. Will that suit you?'

'It sounds good,' Janet nodded.

'Oh, I almost forgot,' Mrs Hammond said suddenly as the three of them surveyed the little lounge-room together, somewhat self-consciously. 'Paul Adams left a message for you.'

'Oh! Where?' Janet looked about her, expecting to see a scribbled note lying on a flat surface somewhere.

It was strange, actually. She wasn't thinking nearly as much about Paul as she would have expected, since recovering from her first disappointment that he had not been at Broken Hill to meet her. He still seemed connected with Sydney somehow, an unreal interlude rather than someone who would figure largely in her new life here.

'Not a written message, dear,' Mrs Hammond explained. 'He rang a couple of hours ago. Said he'd see you on Wednesday evening when you get back from the clinic flight. Sent you his love, though.'

She spoke in the lazy, laconic style of an outback-bred person, and gave the last words no special intonation, but Janet caught Clifford Ransome's sudden cool gaze and was annoyed to find herself flushing.

He disapproved of her relationship with Paul. That was only too clear. She wondered why. Did he think it would interfere with her work? It wouldn't—and it was none of his business anyway.

'Oh, my Lord! I've forgotten the kettle!' Lorna exclaimed just then, and rushed away.

'I'll be going,' Clifford said.

'Of course,' Janet nodded. 'You must be exhausted.'

'I'll see you at seven-fifteen, then.'

He was gone in a moment, without wishing her good night. Janet manufactured a little spurt of anger to quell the unaccountable pang of desolation that had hit her now that she was alone in her new home. She stifled a sigh, then left the small building and walked across to Mrs Hammond's kitchen. It was simply homesickness and tiredness that she was feeling, and it was all perfectly understandable.

CHAPTER THREE

CLIFFORD RANSOME'S knock sounded against the metal screen door at exactly seven-fifteen the next morning. Janet noted the hour on the small travelling alarm clock which had woken her at half past six.

Last night, Lorna Hammond had given her bread, butter, milk and jars of coffee and marmalade for a simple breakfast in her own flat.

'I'll be up just after seven, so I probably won't see you,' the older woman had said.

Janet had spent a restless night in her new bed, but now excitement and apprehension about the two days ahead had her feeling wide awake and ready to absorb a hundred new impressions and experiences.

'Ready?' was Clifford Ransome's economical greeting when she opened the door to him.

'I just need the uniform,' Janet replied, a little embarrassed to be confronting him in her dressing-gown.

It was not modesty, just vanity. She had owned the pale blue chenille gown for years, and although it was clean, it looked distinctly dowdy. He made no sign of noticing her appearance at all, however, but simply handed the sensible white dress to her and stood outside while she changed into it hastily.

When she emerged a few minutes later, she caught his faint approving nod, and her heart lifted a little. Perhaps he would be friendlier today. It really would be preferable if they could get on well. Janet did not like awkward moments, and yesterday there had been too many of them.

'We won't stop and talk to Lorna. I think she's in the shower,' Clifford said, and Janet could hear the sound of

46

water splashing in the bathroom of Mrs. Hammond's quarters too.

She followed Clifford to his four-wheel-drive, and concluded hopefully that he seemed much improved by his night's sleep. Most of the weary irritation and impatience had gone, and she could see now that he was fitter and more athletic than she had thought yesterday. His manner towards her was distant and cool, yet not hostile—which, after all, was exactly what she would expect from a colleague she had met only the day before.

That unexpected thing—the quick moment of flaring sexual awareness between them last night—she refused to think about at all.

Although the air was becoming warmer by the minute, it retained a lingering freshness that was very pleasant, and suddenly Janet was looking forward to the day. Now that she felt awake and alert, she was able to take a lively interest in the town as they drove through it.

There was a general store of modest proportions, the hotel that Clifford had spoken of, a one-roomed school, a small police station, and a church with attached community hall.

'What happens in that hall?' Janet asked cheerfully as they passed it.

'The occasional dance or film screening. The annual church fête.' The words were delivered in a cool matter-of-fact way that put Janet instantly on the defensive and tarnished her morning mood a little.

'I'm not expecting a wild social life, you know,' she blurted out unwisely.

'Did I say I thought you were?' he drawled.

'You looked it.'

He did not reply, but swung the wheel, perhaps more abruptly than he needed to, to bring them to a halt in the parking area at the side of the plain white-painted brick building that was the RFDS Base.

Bill Kirkley was already beside the plane, whose white sides, offset by two horizontal stripes of red and the blue emblem of the RFDS, shone in the morning sun. Brief greetings were exchanged, but little time was wasted.

Equipment and personal bags were stored well down in the tail, then all three climbed aboard, Janet again occupying the small seat in the back of the plane behind the pilot and doctor. She realised as she studied the interior of the plane that she had scarcely absorbed any of its details yesterday.

It was quite cramped, of course, and was beginning to show signs of wear after several years of hard use. Stretchers and other equipment were carefully stored and anchored down in case of bad weather, and the cabin was filled with the sound of the radio tuned to the Flying Doctor frequency.

Dr Ransome turned and passed a somewhat dusty map over to Janet, reeling off the names of the five places they were to visit that day—Patamunda, Franklin's Well, the new gasfields at Tanama where they would have lunch, Diri Diri, and finally their overnight stop at Glencoe Downs. Janet murmured each name softly to herself as she found it on the map. She remembered most of them from her childhood, although she had never been to any of them.

Her mother, and often her father too, had tuned in regularly to the 'Galah' session—the daily exchange of news and gossip which had the transceiver radios on each outback station running hot. The Galah session was named after a rather raucous-voiced pink and grey bird, but the frivolous name belied the importance of this daily event to the people of the outback.

In a region where your nearest neighbour could be well over a hundred miles away, the sense of community and contact established by the radio network was vital, especially to a woman who might have no other company than her husband and small children, and the stockmen who worked on the vast property.

Janet remembered her mother listening avidly to a woman's description of her re-decorating activities in a

homestead 250 miles from their own home, and the tears
of relief and sympathy on her cheeks as she heard of the
safe recovery of a dangerously ill child who lived over
300 miles away.

'Do you find the landscape very harsh?' Dr Ransome
turned to Janet with the question.

'Harsh yes, but very beautiful too,' Janet replied.

'I'm surprised you should think so,' Dr Ransome said.
'Being from the city, I would have thought you'd find it
too savage for your taste.'

Janet bit back a retort and wondered why he seemed
so keen to find her unfit for life out here. He had
obviously discounted a childhood spent in the region. It
was clear that she was going to have to prove herself to
him again and again. She would try hard to do so of
course, but resented his attitude all the same.

She remembered his comments about her hair, and
reached up a hand in a reflex gesture, to pat its neat coils.
She had taken a good fifteen minutes this morning to
plait it into two tight braids then wind them in a golden
halo around the top of her head. It was an old-fashioned
style, and more severe than the ones she usually chose,
yet it suited her well enough, and would certainly keep in
place for the course of the day. Dr Ransome would have
no further cause to comment on it!

A while later, Janet felt a change in the throb of the
aircraft's engine, and realised that they were descending. Bill Kirkley and the doctor had exchanged a few
laconic words on the journey, but the noise of the plane
and of the radio made general conversation directed to
her own seat in the back too difficult.

Their landing was rougher than last night's at
Benanda had been, although Janet thought that the
airstrip on this property was probably better looked-
after than many. She was prepared for the blast of hot air
that struck them as the aircraft's doors were opened, but
hoped that the place where the short clinic was to be held
would turn out to be cool.

A young aboriginal stockman had come out to meet the plane, and as he helped her down onto the ground, Janet experienced a thrill of nerves. Suddenly it was all very real, and she was about to start work.

'Could you tell me what I'll be doing please?' It was an attempt to get herself into her usual mood of practical confidence, but the question, addressed to Clifford Ransome, in her low voice, was still blurted out a little too quickly.

Clifford looked at her for a moment before answering. They were crossing a stretch of bare hard earth to the battered station vehicle that stood waiting for them. The airstrip on this property was nearly a kilometre from the main homestead building, and the drive would be a bumpy one. Janet held one of the bags of equipment and looked at him with disconcerting directness.

She looked small and a little uncertain, but surprisingly cool and capable nonetheless. Apparently, she was undaunted by the heat in her white cotton dress and sandals, even with that heavy coronet of hair, and Clifford was already revising some of his negative preconceptions about her. She might do, she just might—if he could keep her away from too much of Paul Adams' influence, and if that petite prettiness of hers didn't do any damage in other quarters . . .

He closed his mind abruptly against a too-vivid memory from last night—the feeling of that silky ribbon of hair between his fingers.

'Here at Patamunda?' he queried in reply to her question, more tersely than he had intended.

'Yes,' she nodded.

'A few things. Some polio vaccines—there are seven children on this property. And some tetanus boosters to Jock O'Loughlin and two of his stockmen. Mrs O'Loughlin is pregnant and I'll be examining her. One or two more things may turn up. I don't know.'

He saw that Janet nodded calmly at all this, and that she was running quickly through his list in her head, reassuring herself that she would be able to handle it all. She certainly should. It was routine enough.

They bumped along a knife-straight road in the ageing four-wheel-drive. Janet had been given the most comfortable position next to the driver's seat after her back-seat ride in the Piper Chieftain, and the black stockman, although he showed the shyness of a young man brought up away from much contact with strangers, entertained her by pointing out some of the features of the landscape—a few examples of the O'Loughlins' beef cattle herd, a cairn of stones that marked an unknown swagman's grave, and the belt of trees which they were rapidly rearing.

'That's the creek. Seven Mile Creek we call it,' he said. 'Don't know why. It's not seven miles from anything I know.'

The bed of the creek was wide—nearly fifty yards across—and completely dry as most outback creeks were for most of the time. Huge gums with stately white trunks and crowns of foliage in a dozen subtle shades of olive green, purplish pink and amber stood in the coarse sand of the creek-bed and on each bank.

It was a tranquil spot, whose peace was disturbed only by the desultory croak of crows or the screech of sulphur-crested cockatoos. Whoever had built the O'Loughlins' homestead had chosen the site well. It stood on a rise, out of reach of all but the severest floods, but it was close enough to the creek to enjoy the companionship of the trees.

Mrs O'Loughlin was a happy-looking woman of about thirty-five. She greeted the party and gave a welcoming nod to Janet, then accompanied them to the sparsely-furnished but clean room at the end of an outhouse-store that was to be used for the clinic.

Almost immediately, practically everyone on the property had gathered around to wait their turn to see the doctor, or simply to exchange news with Bill, who was at his leisure while the medical team worked.

Clifford and Janet spent a few minutes quickly making the room ready to receive the first patients.

'Here's a packet of barley sugar,' Clifford said, tossing the cellophane-wrapped parcel to Janet, who managed to catch it deftly. 'For the kids if they're good while you give the injections. John Hunt might have something to say about the sugar on his next visit, but you don't want grizzling children on your hands, do you?'

'No, thank you!' Janet laughed. 'But who is John Hunt?'

'The dentist from Broken Hill. He does regular trips around this region, too. He'll probably combine with Paul on the next clinic flight. Ready for our first patients?'

'Ready,' Janet replied, sounding more confident than she felt. What if the children did scream at her ministrations? With all those people gossiping well within earshot on the verandah outside, it would be distinctly embarrassing.

First came the three O'Loughlin children, two sturdy little girls of about six and seven, and a smaller boy who looked about three. They were all fair-haired, freckled and cheerful, and bore their torment with loud but brief 'Ah!'s and 'Ouch!'es, then accepted their barley sugars and were shepherded off again to begin their morning lessons with the School of the Air.

Meanwhile, Dr Ransome was giving the more painful tetanus boosters to Jock O'Loughlin and two of the aboriginal stockmen that worked the station, each of whom gave merely a stoical grimace.

There was not much privacy to the whole operation, Janet reflected. While she had been immunising the O'Loughlin children, two aboriginal women had arrived with their offspring, from their small settlement which lay beyond the homestead and nearer to the creek. The four children, aged between one and five, were shy of the new nurse at first, but Janet drew their attention and interest by chatting about some of the equipment in the room and was rewarded when, like the little O'Loughlins, they merely stiffened and gave one squawk and whimper of pain as the injection was given.

Clifford had already finished his job, and went out on to the verandah where he had a quick look at a couple more problems. One was a gash in one of the stockmen's hands that had been infected on the medical team's last routine visit, but which was now nicely healed thanks to the antiseptic powder which Clifford had prescribed. The other, a persistent weepy eye in one of the aboriginal women, gave him more concern and he told her to report back to him over the radio transceiver within the next few days if the treatment he prescribed did not cure it.

'You'd rather be examined in the house, wouldn't you, Mrs O'Loughlin?' Clifford asked when both he and Janet had finished with the other patients.

She nodded, and they walked across together from the outbuilding.

'How about a cool drink before you go?' Jock O'Loughlin said, so Janet and Bill followed him to the house too, through a dry-soiled but shrub-filled garden.

Mrs O'Loughlin was in fine health in the middle of her fourth month of pregnancy, so they had only just finished glasses of tart and icy lime juice cordial when the doctor emerged from his examination and it was time to go, bouncing back to the plane again in the station vehicle.

'They take the RFDS very much for granted these days, don't they?' Janet commented to Dr Ransome as they walked to the plane.

'Yes, they do,' he said. 'Do you think that's wrong?'

'I didn't say that.' She reacted to what she felt was a challenging note in his tone.

'Medical services are taken for granted in the city, too,' Clifford said, ignoring her protest. 'To me, it proves that the Service is effective. It's an integral part of outback life in every way, and that is exactly what John Flynn dreamt of all those years when he was trying to establish it.'

'It was quite an achievement, wasn't it?'

'It was. It still is. I'm proud to be a part of it—though of course there are those god-awful days when I wish I had a nice private specialist's practice in Sydney.'

He frowned suddenly and Janet wondered guiltily if yesterday had been one of those days.

After that first visit, the day seemed to whizz by, leaving Janet with an array of first impressions which would be a blur when she looked back on them in days to come. Their second stop, Franklin's Well, was a marked contrast to the first. In her practical way, Janet took in the desolate and run-down buildings of the small homestead, noticed that an attempt at creating a garden had been abandoned years ago, and wondered how people managed to live like this without a single tree for shade —not to mention for beauty.

There were no children on the place—little human company at all, in fact—but Mrs Franklin did not betray any discontent, apart from a few words about the 'female troubles' which Dr Ransome discussed with her and prescribed some medicine for.

They had a quick cup of tea at Franklin's Well, and Fred and Jean Franklin both soaked up Benanda gossip avidly, then the team had to be on its way, as they were expected for lunch at the Tanama gasfields. They would probably have a good few patients amongst the fifty-odd men who worked there in dramatic and purely masculine isolation.

It was four o'clock when they reached Diri Diri, after a smorgasbord lunch in the cafeteria in the Tanama men's quarters, and a busy session of check-ups and minor medical repairs.

'Just in time for afternoon tea,' said Frank Beddie, Diri Diri's owner, after they had stepped out of the plane and Janet had been introduced.

'Great!' was Clifford Ransome's hearty reply. Actually, the reply was rather too hearty, Janet decided. There was something false about the doctor's manner. She did not know him well, yet, but she had already formed the impression that he was not effusive or over-enthusiastic in his dealings with people.

The two men had shaken hands energetically and actually patted each other on the back as an additional greeting, yet their smiles did not quite reach their eyes, and they avoided each other's direct gaze. Janet could sense a distinct tension in the air, and heard Bill whistle a bubble-gum pop song tunelessly at her side, as if he, too, were trying to cover up an undercurrent of feelings with the uncharacteristic sound.

Both the doctor and the station owner were talkative as they walked to the homestead, which was a cool-looking and gracious old building, with a wooden-floored verandah and screened-in walkways leading to outhouses and sheds. Dr Ransome kept up a continuous series of questions about the state of the herd, the state of the market, the state of the station water-supply . . .

Janet's uneasiness grew. It sounded as if the doctor was afraid of a silence falling between himself and Frank Beddie. Could it simply be that they disliked one another? Surely not. That wasn't the way Dr Ransome would behave with someone he disliked. Janet had no good reason for being so sure of that, but she *was* sure of it just the same.

'Was that a lake I could see not far from here as we were coming in to land, Dr Ransome? Or just a mirage?' Janet said, wanting to break the too-hearty flow of conversation if she could.

She knew perfectly well that it was a lake, a salt lake. She had seen it on the map, but he would not know that.

'A lake,' the doctor turned to her, with relief replacing the hunted look in his brown eyes.

'I thought it must have been.' She threw him a smile, meeting his gaze frankly, and he smiled back.

For a second, it was as if she could see clearly straight into his thoughts, and she knew that his strange manner with Frank Beddie had its source in a part of his past that was still very important to him. Important and . . . painful? The moment of revelation passed, and she could not tell.

'I'll put the kettle on right now,' Frank Beddie said as they entered the house. 'There's no cake. I'm afraid. A few biscuits . . . I think they're a bit stale. Perhaps you'd like to set up your gear while the water boils. Spare bedroom do you? Like last time?'

'Absolutely fine, absolutely fine,' Clifford nodded, still speaking with forced and uncharacteristic cheerfulness.

'I might skip the tea and take a dip instead if that's all right with you, Cliff,' Bill said quietly.

'Yes, go ahead,' the doctor replied absently.

'Got a towel I could borrow, Frank?'

'Sure . . . somewhere,' Frank said. Janet suppressed a smile. The man appeared to live in bachelor chaos.

'You might get a leech or two,' Frank said when he had produced the big scratchy towel after a careless search.

'Won't worry me,' was Bill's laconic assurance.

He went off straight away, and Janet followed him with her gaze as he walked the two hundred yards to the belt of trees that marked the Nardoo River, which at this spot had a water-hole that was almost never dry. And it would certainly be deep and long this year after the plentiful rains of the last few seasons.

'Stephanie is coming back just before Christmas.' Frank broke a stiff silence ten minutes later as the three sat in a comparatively cool spot on the verandah.

After their initial fevered conversation, the two men had seemed to run out of steam, and Janet herself had come to the end of her repertoire of questions about the property. She wasn't by any means a chatter-box and had found it an effort.

'Before *Christmas*!' Clifford sounded more than surprised.

'It was her idea,' Frank said gruffly and defensively.

'Yes, but . . .' Clifford began abruptly, then stopped and continued more gently. 'Perhaps you should have tried to talk her out of it.'

'I didn't want to,' Frank said. 'It'll be good to have her here. It's her place to be here. Mum and my brother and sister-in-law are driving over from Innabandina. It'll be good to have her here with the family.'

'Yes, of course.'

Janet could see that Clifford was biting back a longer and angrier reply. She had to fight a growing curiosity, telling herself that it was none of her business. She wasn't someone who took a prurient interest in other people's affairs. All the same, she wouldn't be able to help finding out more eventually, when she had been in the district longer. Or perhaps Clifford himself would say something when they were on the plane again. Was Stephanie Frank Beddie's wife? His sister?

'How is your Ventilin supply,' Clifford was saying now in his most professional tone.

'Pretty low,' Frank Beddie replied.

'Still having a lot of attacks?'

'Yes. It gives me the sh . . .' he bit off the last word, glanced, embarrassed, at Janet, then continued. 'Don't know what's causing them half the time. It was all right for a good while back there.'

'It's to be expected, actually,' Clifford said. 'Asthma doesn't only have physical causes, you know. I've got some Ventilin . . . Damn! I left it in the plane.'

'I'll get it,' Janet put in quickly.

The airstrip at Diri Diri was within easy walking distance of the homestead. It would be a hot two hundred yards there and back, but at least she would be able to escape from the strange thread of tension between these men.

'Will you be able to find it?' Clifford asked, frowning.

'Yes, I noticed it among some other things while we were at Tanama,' Janet answered him, noticing the jerky movement of one long trouser-clad leg as he tapped his foot tensely.

'Take your hat,' he said.

The advice was sound. Heat pressed down on her like a weight. It even seemed to make breathing more difficult, Janet noticed. The air was bone dry, and the horizon shimmered in loose waves. Janet found the Ventilin with no trouble, and when she returned, the tea-tray had gone from the verandah.

She could hear the voices of the two men coming from inside the house, however, and they were voices raised in anger.

'You think you know what's best for her.' It was Frank. 'But she's my wife. She's with *me* now, and we'll decide together.'

'Do you think it'll be any different—' Clifford's words broke off abruptly and he gave a rasping sigh.

'You're using the fact that you're a doctor. You're pretending to be uninvolved, but don't think that I'm . . .'

'That's absurd. Look, please try to calm down.' Clifford lowered his voice.

Janet had stopped at the door after one step onto the wooden threshhold, and was about to retreat, but she realised now that they had heard her. She felt suddenly drained, sweating after the exertion of the hot walk, and unequal to the task of facing the two angry men and pretending that nothing was wrong. They knew she was there, but she didn't care, and turned hard on her heel to find peace and solitude in the rough garden between the side of the homestead and the storage outbuildings. Clifford could come and find her if he wanted her.

He did come, about ten minutes later. Janet heard his footsteps on the baked earth and his clear-toned voice calling her name quietly. For a moment, she hid shamelessly behind a white-flowered oleander bush, afraid that he would be angry with her, but then she realised that if he was, he would only be more so as time passed.

'I'm here.' She stepped out to where he could see her, furious to discover that she felt quite weak. It was largely the heat, no doubt.

He wasn't angry. Or at least, if he was, he concealed it well.

'Got the Ventilin?'

'Yes. Here.' She held out a hand that was distinctly damp and met the touch of his own warm fingers for an instant as he took the small package from her.

'Stay here if you like,' he said. 'Or find some shade by the river. I've only got three people to see. It'll take about fifteen minutes, probably, and I don't need you.'

'Okay,' she nodded, and he left her to herself again. Obviously there was to be no explanation of the scene that had just occurred. Perhaps she didn't even want one.

It was later than planned when they arrived at Glencoe Downs, where they were to spend the night. Dr Ransome frowned when he saw the big group of people waiting to see him. Glencoe Downs was a huge well-run property, with a large aboriginal settlement about ten miles from the main homestead. Two car-loads of the settlement's inhabitants had driven the distance especially for the clinic, and they would have to be seen tonight, even if some of the homestead people waited until tomorrow morning.

This time there was no question of Janet taking no part in consultations. She worked busily for more than an hour in a small room adjoining the larger space where Dr Ransome had set out his equipment. There were more vaccinations to perform, then a bad cut to clean and bandage.

'Thought I'd see what happened if I just left it,' the stockman explained, wincing as Janet probed at the nasty wound and extracted several pieces of grit.

'It's slightly infected,' she cautioned the sun-burnished man. 'So make sure you change the dressing as I've told you and keep using that powder.'

'Yeah . . . if I remember,' he growled, and she made a mental note to get Clifford to follow up the case during his routine radio consultations over the coming week.

It was after seven when Clifford poked his head around the door and told her that he was about to see the last of his waiting patients.

'I'll only be ten minutes,' he said. 'Tidy up when you've finished with Albert here, then come in next door.'

Janet nodded and he went out again. His manner had softened and warmed since the tense time at Diri Diri. Perhaps he was trying to make up for it in some way.

When Janet joined him several minutes later, he was just saying goodbye to the old aboriginal woman he had been examining. When the woman left and they were alone, he stretched his back muscles and loosened the collar of his white shirt with a lean hand.

'Long day,' he said.

'Yes,' Janet nodded.

'Enjoyed it?' He looked at her in his direct way.

'I have.'

'Different from what you expected, perhaps.'

Janet stiffened a little. 'Not really, no.' She was answering the question truthfully, but her awareness of why he had asked it made her tone a little defensive. For a moment he looked sceptical and she was about to comment on it but he spoke again.

'Anyway, you've worked well. I'm very pleased.'

Clifford emphasised the words as much as he could. He wasn't a man who found it easy or liked to give fulsome praise. He preferred to convey things like that in subtler ways—by some added courtesy, by a practical demonstration of trust.

But he wanted to find a way of apologising for making her . . . play gooseberry, you could almost call it . . .

between himself and Frank Beddie this afternoon. He also wanted to apologise for the fact that he wasn't going to tell her anything about the affair. It was a medical matter, in many ways, so he *should* tell her. But it was a very personal one, too, and to talk about it, even clinically as a 'case', would require too great a betrayal of himself. So he took refuge in this way of making it up to her.

She *had* worked well today, very well. He just hoped that her dedication wouldn't wear thin under Paul Adams' influence. He couldn't help fearing that it would. After all, the girl had dropped everything at short notice to come up here to be with the junior doctor.

Clifford looked at her. A faint flush of pleasure glowed on her cheeks at his compliment and she was thanking him, her grey-green eyes alight. He could see quite clearly why Paul's fickle attention had been drawn to the girl.

'Don't thank me,' he said, quite brusquely now. 'Just see that you keep it up. Especially when Paul Adams is around.'

There! He had spoiled the compliment now, but it had to be said, he told himself, burying a tinge of regret and uncertainty. She had turned away from him now.

'Do we put this equipment back in the plane?' she asked in a coolly matter-of-fact tone.

'No. It stays in here overnight. I've got the key to the room. We've still got a few people to see tomorrow before we leave.'

'That's right. I'd forgotten.' Her tone was still carefully neutral, but Clifford could see that she wanted to make a retort to his attack about Paul. She didn't make it, though, which made him think that the shaft had gone home.

He was suddenly annoyed about the whole thing. A doctor had enough emotional complications to deal with amongst his patients—like at Diri Diri!—without finding them amongst his staff as well. If only he could find some nice, safe older married woman for the nursing job—'one that wouldn't arouse your interest, not just Paul's', a small voice said inside him. He ignored it.

'We should get across to the house,' he said to Janet. 'They'll be holding dinner and I need a shower first. I daresay you do too.'

Janet walked ahead of the doctor, unsettled by what had just passed between them. It was clear, now, how much Clifford Ransome mistrusted her relationship with Paul, and she couldn't decide what to do about it. One part of her wanted to say to Clifford that Paul was just a friend, or that, at any rate, she had no intention of responding seriously to his interest in her and he had had nothing to do with her reasons for taking this job.

But another stubborner part felt differently. Her relationship with Paul was none of this man's business, and it was insulting that he didn't believe she would be able to maintain a clear line between work and personal life. She wasn't going to go crawling to him with explanations. She would just quietly and thoroughly prove him wrong.

At this decision, she gave a proud lift to her chin and quickened her pace, filled with new energy now that the draining heat of the day was dissipating. She reached the screen door of the homestead ahead of him and held it open, meeting his surprised gaze with a confident challenging smile—whose effect was a little lessened, admittedly, by the fact that she had to look up so far to allow for his height.

'After you, Dr Ransome,' she said.

CHAPTER FOUR

IT was cool on the verandah of the guest outhouse at Glencoe Downs station. The sun had well and truly set, and crickets sang from some hidden place, as if welcoming the new freshness in the air.

Janet intended to be in bed within ten minutes, but first she had to complete the nightly ritual of brushing her hair. She had skipped it last night, for once, and had not had time to comb out all the accumulated tangles this morning, so that when she unbraided the tight plaits, there was a fair collection of knots. It was lucky that it was thick and straight enough not to tangle too readily, and she usually enjoyed the rhythmic task of brushing and combing.

Tonight, as there was no one about, she stood on the verandah to do it, drinking in the scents of the night and identifying the pattern of the stars which shone out with great brightness here in the desert, having no competition from other light as they did in the city.

Clifford Ransome was staying in the next room, and Bill Kirkley was in the last one at the far end of the verandah, but they were both still involved in conversation with Mr and Mrs Henry and their two grown-up but unmarried sons.

Janet relished such moments of solitude, and was startled when this one was interrupted suddenly.

'I see that Rapunzel has let down her hair.'

'Rapunzel is getting the tangles out, and it's taking a long time,' Janet laughed in her low voice.

Immediately, she was sorry she had made the response. Clifford had been quietly friendly to her over dinner, but he would be bound to use her words as the cue for another reminder about cutting off her beloved tresses. He didn't, though.

'May I help?' The softly voiced question took her aback, and her reply was clumsy.

'I . . . I suppose so.'

She glanced at him uncertainly. He stood leaning against the verandah post quite close to her. He had changed after his shower into a khaki shirt of soft cotton and pants of a slightly darker shade. His brown neck rose from a collar that was open, and his sleeves were rolled to just below the elbow, revealing tanned and muscular forearms. There was moonlight, and his dark eyes glinted warmly in it as their gaze met.

He stepped forward, and the wooden verandah creaked. Why hadn't she heard those creaks in the first place as he approached, and gone into her room before he could speak to her? With its tensions, flaring antagonisms and sudden moments of gentleness, their relationship was rapidly becoming too complex for comfort.

But when he took the brush and comb from her hand, Janet made no protest. There was an old armchair on the verandah which he pulled forward and sat down in, so that by reaching up, he could get to the full length of her hair's golden sweep without having to change position. First, he deftly found the knots that remained and teased them out, as gentle as he would have been if he had been removing a splinter from a child's foot. Then he used the brush with rhythmic sweeping strokes, finding the strong pressure she liked as if by instinct.

Fuzzy shivers played up and down the length of her spine and tingled in her scalp. She closed her eyes to enjoy it more, then felt him put the brush down. His fingers, cool and firm, came to the sides of her face, sending a sudden pulse of awareness coursing through her body. He shaped her hair back into a single rope, then he stood up and lifted the mass of it, burying his face in its fragrant coils.

'It smells of balsam,' he said. 'And dust.'

'Oh, tremendous!'

'Just a bit. It's quite a nice combination.'

He reached out a hand and turned her to face him. Her hair was still lifted in the other hand, but then he let it fall slowly, all to one side over her right shoulder. They were standing very close—although she only came to his chest—and in another moment she knew that the magnetic tension between them would erupt into a kiss. She was on the point of swaying towards him and saw the smouldering fire in his eyes, but then voices came out of the darkness.

''Night, Tom!'

''Night, Bill. Sleep well . . .'

For a second, Janet felt the touch of Clifford's parted lips against her own, then Bill Kirkley's heavy footsteps on the wooden verandah shattered the mood, and seconds later he was beside them. Clifford had already retreated to a safe distance.

'Gazing at the stars, you two?'

They both laughed awkwardly, then Bill whistled as he caught sight of Janet's cascade of hair.

'Didn't realise it was *that* long,' he said. 'Must be a job to look after it. Anyway, I'm going to hit the hay.'

'Yes . . . me too,' Clifford said. 'You'd better, as well, Janet. We have another long day tomorrow.'

'Of course, yes,' she murmured, not knowing if she was glad or sorry that Bill had arrived when he did.

Clifford's tone had been very stiff just then. Probably he was already regretting that he had so nearly given way to the impulse which had seized them both. He was at the door of his room already. Glad or sorry? Janet decided firmly that she was glad.

The next day, a hotter one if anything, they visited four more properties and dealt with a similar series of routine problems. The insidious magic of last night's calm and moonlit evening had vanished in the glare of the day, and Janet found it hard to believe that

the shared awareness between herself and Clifford
Ransome had really happened. Very likely it had all
been in her imagination, or in the potency of the large
glass of beer she had been offered before dinner, she
decided sensibly.

Clifford's manner towards her certainly betrayed no
new softness, and he seemed once again like a stranger.

Janet doubted her perceptions about his tension at
Diri Diri too. It was silly to read any mystery into what
was probably just plain dislike between two strong-
willed men. Perhaps it was the heat that made some
emotions seem stronger, more violent, and more sharply
delineated. Janet did not enjoy mulling over people's
quirks of behaviour, so she wasn't going to keep on
puzzling about Clifford Ransome. She felt that she knew
most of what she needed to know about him already, and
this seemed to be confirmed by the fact that they worked
quite well together throughout the day. Dr Ransome
liked his nurses to keep to impersonal topics of conversation, it seemed, and Janet found it quite easy to
oblige.

It was six in the evening by the time they arrived back
at Benanda, and no time was wasted in collecting their
personal luggage and preparing to go home. Janet could
see that Clifford Ransome was thinking of his tranquil
verandah and a cool drink. She wondered if he spent all
of his evenings alone, and if he preferred it that way.

For her own part, she was looking forward to getting
to know Lorna Hammond better, but hoped for a good
hour of solitary reading in bed followed by a long quiet
night's sleep as well.

Two people stood waiting on the side verandah of the
Flying Doctor Base that looked out on to the airstrip.
One of them was Paul.

Janet recognised him with quite a shock. Two days
ago she had been longing to see him—a comparatively
familiar face in this new world. But the events and
impressions that had been crammed into the last forty-

eight hours had pushed her thoughts of Paul very much
into the background.

That week of seeing him in Sydney seemed a long time
ago now, and her memory of the relationship they had
formed was mixed up with all sorts of other memories
now—the shared excitement and hilarity of passing the
midwifery course, the hum of change in the air, the
vibrance of late spring, too, Janet had a sudden fear that
Paul would not find the same frivolous mood in her
now . . .

'You look hot and sticky,' was his first comment as he
stepped off the verandah and gathered her in a tight
squeeze that left her breathless. 'You *feel* hot and sticky,
too.'

He loosened his hold, then planted a deliberate kiss
on her lips. Janet made a token response, but felt too
tired to be enthusiastic. In any case, she wasn't a particularly demonstrative person, and would rather save her
kisses for another time, when they were alone. Was that
unfair? She didn't want to have to worry about it.

Out of the corner of her eye, she saw that Clifford had
arrived on the verandah now too. Paul tossed him a light
greeting, still holding Janet firmly to him. It seemed
quite impossible to think that last night she had almost
been in Clifford's arms like this.

'Quite a welcoming committee for a routine flight,'
the junior doctor quipped.

'Yes, it does seem a bit excessive,' Clifford said drily.

Janet looked at the other member of the 'committee',
able to get a clear impression of her for the first time now
that Paul's broad torso was not blocking her view.

'I'm surprised that you came, Marcia,' Dr Ransome
was saying to her.

'Of course I came,' the girl said. 'I wanted to see you.
And in any case, I was bored at home. I took Mum's car
and she says I don't have to have it back till eleven.'

Marcia was very young. Janet could see that at once,
not only from her appearance, but from the lack of finish

to her coquettish gestures. She was very pretty, with blue eyes, tanned skin, and sun-bleached hair, and her slim figure was shown to advantage in its tight-fitting cream canvas jeans, smart tan riding boots and crimson singlet-top. She wore heavy eye make-up, and her bright earrings jangled under the effect of her restless energy.

'Aren't you going to kiss me?' she pouted teasingly, raising herself on to her toes to reach Clifford's face, without giving him time to take any initiative.

Janet saw him smile then press his lips against Marcia's blonde hair and wide brown forehead, and she felt a sudden prick of irritation, mingled with another emotion that she could not define. But Paul was claiming her attention again.

'Feel like hitting the town tonight?'

'Hitting the town?' Janet laughed. 'I don't mean to sound rude, but . . . what is there to hit?'

'Don't forget that Lorna Hammond probably has dinner prepared for you, Janet.' Clifford's cool tone cut in as soon as she had finished speaking. Paul looked annoyed at the reminder.

'She wouldn't mind,' he said.

'Perhaps not, but it would be a courtesy to let her know of your plans.' Clifford directed the reply at Janet.

'Of course.' Janet, like Paul, was annoyed, but for a different reason. She had thought of Mrs Hammond, too, and had had no intention of simply going off with Paul for the evening, but Clifford had jumped quickly to the wrong conclusion.

'I suppose you're the new nurse,' blonde-haired Marcia put in, deflecting the tension before it was resolved.

'Yes, I am. My name's Janet Green.' Janet turned to the girl, not warming to her particularly, but glad of a chance to forget her irritation with both of Benanda's doctors.

'I'm Marcia Fairfax,' was the reply. 'I live out at

Fairwater Park, about fifteen miles from town—if you can call this place a town. I'll be seeing you around anyway. Let's go, Cliff!' She caught at his hand confidently and he seemed happy to follow.

'Yes . . . See you,' Janet managed, but the pair were already on their way.

She realised too late that there were several things she had meant to ask Clifford. What would be her hours over the next few days, for example, and what happened when she was on call for emergency work? Still, Paul would presumably know.

'What about a picnic by the river?' he was saying, claiming her attention again.

'I really don't think I should, Paul,' Janet answered him seriously. 'Clifford was right. I've barely met Mrs Hammond. She'll have dinner for me, as he said, and it's a good opportunity for us to get to know each other . . .'

'You have to come for a drink, at least,' Paul cut across her last words impatiently.

'I don't *have* to,' Janet retorted, wondering why she was suddenly feeling this irritation with Paul.

'Hey! What's the matter with you?' Paul said, taken aback.

'I'm tired. Can't you see that?' Janet said.

'Yeah, all right,' he nodded.

'I will have a drink though,' Janet said hastily, suddenly suspecting that she had snapped at him more than she should have.

'Good. Lorna eats at seven-ish. I'll get you home by then. Let's put that in the car and get going.' He nodded at the overnight bag she had placed on the ground beside her.

Janet followed him to the car, trying to summon some enthusiasm, but finding it very difficult. She had not slept very well the night before at Glencoe Downs, and the past two days had both been very long ones. She thought suddenly and unexpectedly of Clifford Ransome's quiet plant-filled verandah and the hour or so she had spent on it reading and eating without having to pretend to a gaiety and liveliness that she did not feel. It was hard to imagine Paul enjoying that sort of evening.

Actually, it was hard to imagine Marcia being content with it either. The girl was obviously itching for a wider social life. Janet wondered how she and Clifford would spend their time tonight. As Paul manoeuvred his car out of the Flying Doctor Base car-park, Janet managed to take a look at the senior doctor's nearby house.

Its doors and windows were open, and the sound of rock music came loudly through the still-warm air. Janet saw Marcia come out on to the screened-in verandah with a tray of drinks, singing a snatch of the rock song in an exuberant but not very tuneful voice.

'Short memory, must have a sho-o-ort memory— Clifford, can I feed the goldfish?'

Then Paul's car sped up and they moved out of sight and sound of the doctor's house. It was obvious that Clifford Ransome did not always want only silence and his own company in the evenings.

The drink at the Drover's Dream Hotel was pleasant enough. Janet enjoyed her lime and bitters, but found that the rather rough atmosphere of the bar grated on her tired nerves tonight. For Paul's sake, she tried to be lively, however, and used the opportunity to ask about duty hours and on-call time.

'You're on call virtually all the time, since you're the only nurse,' Paul informed her. 'But don't worry. The hours tend to average out all right. You may get a run of bad days, but then there will be a quiet spell. I don't suppose you've done on-call work before?'

'No,' Janet replied. 'It's not something nurses have to do very often.'

'The worst part is the phone going off by your bed in the middle of the night,' Paul said. 'You jerk awake in an instant. It must be terrible for the central nervous system!'

Janet laughed and noted that he looked pleased. She

wished she could get over this feeling of being so distant from him, as though he was part of another life.

'I won't come in,' he said as they parted in front of Mrs Hammond's a little later. 'Lorna will probably have the meal on the table already, but I'll see you tomorrow when you're in to write up the notes from the clinic flight.'

'I'll be in a more interesting mood then,' she promised.

'Oh, you're interesting now,' he assured her. 'I'm just not quite sure how alive you are. Let's find out, shall we?'

He leaned towards her teasingly after the last comment, intending to find her lips, but she turned her head and gave him her cheek instead.

'Not tonight, Paul.'

'Any reason?'

'I don't know. Tiredness. Let's not make a big thing of it.'

'Well, what's left then? Good night, I suppose,' he smiled, covering his annoyance.

'Yes, good night, Paul.'

He drove off straight away, accelerating rapidly and sending up clouds of dust as he turned on the red dirt verge of the road. Janet felt a helpless frustration, knowing that she had alienated Paul, but telling herself that she did not owe him anything, and he should understand if the past two days had left her a little spiritless.

Shrugging off the whole thing, Janet went inside to greet Lorna Hammond. A plain but tasty dinner of chicken, chips and salad was just about ready, and Lorna seemed happy to do most of the talking over the meal. She was a strongly-built woman with iron-grey hair, full of a somewhat clumsy energy and cheerfulness. Clearly, she enjoyed the opportunity for contact with people that her service station gave her, and was full of interesting anecdotes, to which Janet only had to reply briefly.

It was only half past eight when Lorna put down her empty tea-cup.

'I'm sure you need an early bed, so don't feel you have to sit and yabber with me all night,' she said. 'You've probably still got unpacking to do, too.'

'Yes, I have,' Janet nodded, putting down her empty cup too. 'It's been a bit of an unsettling start, going away on the clinic flight after arriving so late on Sunday. It'll be nice to spend the rest of the evening settling in better.'

'Off you go, then,' Mrs Hammond nodded. 'But just come over and ask if there's anything you need, and I'll see what I can do.'

By the end of the first week, Wednesday's feeling of dislocation and tiredness had passed, and life in Benanda was already falling into a routine that was pleasant if mostly quiet. Janet had written up the notes from the clinic flight, listened in to Paul's morning radio consultation, and attended two emergencies with Dr Ransome, both of which had ended satisfactorily.

There had been no hint in his behaviour towards her of the kind of awareness that had flared between them at Glencoe Downs. Janet behaved in a strictly business-like way too, feeling that he was still testing her capabilities in the new job. Bill Kirkley's presence and his laconic country-bred humour made things a lot easier. The Base's second pilot, who had made one of the emergency flights with them, was a nice enough character too, although a bit taciturn.

Janet was finding out more about the town and its inhabitants as the days passed. Marcia Fairfax, she discovered, belonged to the district's best-known family, whose property, Fairwater Park, was both prosperous and well-run. It had been in the family now for several generations, and the Fairfax clan thought of themselves as something akin to the gentry of the region.

Marcia herself, the eldest daughter of Kevin Fairfax who owned the property with his brother Francis, was only eighteen and had finished her studies at a girls' boarding school in Adelaide just over a year ago. It was clear that she was bored out at Fairwater Park, as she did not take much of an interest in work around the station, as her younger sister and brothers did. Janet wondered whether her feelings for Clifford Ransome were serious, or whether he just provided some interest in her days.

She wondered more about the senior doctor's feelings for Marcia. He must be at least thirty. Not an enormous age-gap between them, of course, but even leaving that aside, did they have much in common?

Still, it was no concern of hers, she told herself more than once that week when Marcia came into the Flying Doctor Base in search of Clifford. Janet wished that Clifford would reach the same conclusion about herself and Paul Adams. She was aware of the senior doctor's veiled hostility and disapproval every time he saw Paul at her side. It made it all the harder to work out her own attitude to her relationship with Paul.

She had been to the hotel with him twice more for drinks, and had sheltered from Saturday afternoon's heat at his modest one-bedroomed house, listening to records and chatting. They had even tried a game of tennis after six on Sunday evening at the rather run-down court behind the church, but Janet had found it too hot. Tennis was a winter sport in Benanda. Paul had not coaxed her into any greater physical intimacy, but she could tell that he was just biding his time, and tried to work out what her response would be. His light-hearted company was helping her to settle in here, but how did she really feel about him?

'What about a picnic tea tomorrow night?' he said to her on Wednesday afternoon a week after her return from the clinic flight, coming up to her while she was checking over lists of medical supplies.

Dr Ransome was well within earshot, having just poured himself coffee after finishing a long emergency radio consultation about a child who had burnt its hand.

It had been one of those difficult times when he had not been quite sure about his decision not to fly out to the accident, and this was having an effect on his mood, Janet could clearly see.

'A picnic would be good,' Janet said.

'By the river,' Paul elaborated. 'You haven't been there yet, have you? We'll swim, unless water the colour of weak tea puts you off too much.'

'I've swum in worse,' Janet smiled back.

Clifford Ransome was listening to their conversation. He could not help doing so, of course, being in the same room, but he didn't have to radiate his disapproval so clearly. Anyway, what was wrong with a picnic tea? Did the man want to have complete control over the lives of his staff? Or was it something special about herself and Paul?

The river was about ten minutes drive from town, down a winding dirt road which was very dusty at this time of year. Janet had not been called out that day, and it was her first real chance to spend time settling into her room and exploring the little town. She met Paul for a drink at the hotel at five, and they lingered over it so that it was nearly six by the time they arrived at the town's most popular picnic spot.

Only one other car was there, but Janet was disconcerted to discover that it was Dr Ransome's. Perhaps that was why he had looked so unusually annoyed when he heard her make the arrangement with Paul? He had hoped to be alone with Marcia Fairfax at the tranquil spot which was upstream from the girl's own home.

Marcia had spread a large towel out on a sloping grass-covered place on the bank and was lazing on it, her face shaded by a wide-brimmed hat and her eyes concealed by sunglasses. She was watching Clifford, who swam energetically, clearly enjoying the cool water. Janet had been looking forward to a swim very much herself, but now that he was here she felt reluctant. Did he want to be left alone in the water?

No, that was ridiculous. Their relationship wasn't that strained! She had come for a swim and a meal with Paul and she would enjoy these things regardless. Clifford was heading towards the far bank now. If she entered the water straight away, she would have claimed some space in it with Paul before he returned.

Quickly, Janet slipped out of her cream sundress to reveal a smart swimming costume of pink, turquoise and blue. She tested the water with one foot before turning to call to Paul that the water seemed fine. She was surprised to find that he had laid out his towel near Marcia's and was clearly planning to sun himself on it for a while before entering the water.

'You're not coming in, Paul?'

'I'll work my way up to it. Got to get in a bit of tanning first,' he grinned.

'That's a nice costume, Janet,' Marcia called lazily. 'From Sydney, I suppose. It'll get ruined by our water.'

'I'd rather ruin a swimming costume than go without a swim,' Janet replied.

Marcia never seemed to have a good word to say about her home town. She was clearly very restless and unhappy here, and Janet wondered if she was hoping to move to Sydney with Clifford Ransome, and enjoy the far more cosmopolitan lifestyle of a doctor's wife. Paul was chatting to Marcia now, leaving Janet to enter the water by herself.

She did so, wincing at its comparative chill at first, but soon finding it a perfect temperature after the hot day. Clifford was still near the far bank, swimming around in a small area as if testing the water for something.

A minute later, he got out onto the bank, water streaming from his tanned body and black swimming briefs. Then he began to climb a big tree that hung over the water. On looking more closely, Janet could see that someone had nailed pieces of wood up the trunk to form a rough ladder. Clifford was heading for a wide flat branch about fifteen feet above the water.

He was going to dive! She realised it just a moment before he made the movement, curving down gracefully and hitting the water with an economical splash. Janet had breast-stroked out towards the middle and could see his expression of satisfaction as he surfaced again.

'Beautiful!' she called out, thinking that she might as well be sociable in spite of the uncertainty that she felt whenever she was with him—except when they could both take refuge in talking about work.

'Thanks!' he called back. 'I'm going to try another one.'

This time it was a swan dive, as well-executed as the last had been. It was clearly something he did often and enjoyed very much.

'That was even better,' she said, when his head emerged from the water only feet from her.

'Why don't you try one?' he said. 'It's perfectly safe. I've made a thorough check for snags and the water is very deep at this spot.'

'Oh, I couldn't!'

'But you seem to be a strong swimmer. What about a jump, if you're afraid to dive?'

'But . . .'

'Go on. I can never get Marcia to do anything interesting in the water. I'll come up with you to give you moral support, if you like.'

They hung suspended in the slow current, both lazily treading water to keep afloat. Clifford seemed unusually relaxed, as if this was, like his tranquil house, a place where he could forget both his work and any problems in his personal life. His wet hair was a mess, as dishevelled as a boy's, and his tanned limbs moved capably.

Suddenly, Janet felt as if they were just children and playmates. Tensions about Paul and Marcia vanished. Being here in the water with Clifford was surprisingly good.

'All right. I'll do it,' she said impulsively.

They both struck out for the bank in a quick crawl. He left the water first and climbed up the tree ladder, his brown toes curling around its rungs confidently. At the top he turned around and reached down to her, realising that the climb would be harder for someone of her height.

Janet grasped his cool wet hand firmly and was soon beside him on the wide horizontal branch, but the water looked a long way down from here, and she couldn't help being a bit afraid. He saw it.

'It's not easy the first time,' Clifford said. 'I think I would have chickened out if some ten year olds hadn't been watching my every move!'

'I might climb down again.'

'No, you don't.' He was laughing but insistent. 'That's much harder than jumping. Hold my hand and we'll jump together . . . only remember to hold your nose with the other hand!'

He had stood up, steadying himself by reaching up a muscled arm to hold on to a higher branch above his head, and now he coaxed her to her feet too, giving her no time to reconsider, but taking her hand deliberately.

'Here we go . . .'

'No!'

'Yes!'

They hit the water together in an exhilarating rush and when Janet came to the surface she was laughing aloud.

'Fabulous!'

'Again?' he asked, grinning broadly. What was it that stopped him from being like this more often?

'Oh . . . Yes!'

'By yourself?'

'I think so.'

Paul and Marcia were still lazing on the bank when Janet swam over after two more jumps. She was feeling water-logged but happy in the special way that comes after shared physical fun with someone. It was very surprising that she had found such a feeling with Clifford.

'We've got to go, Cliff,' Marcia called out as soon as the doctor was within easy earshot. 'Mum said dinner at half past seven, and we'll be late if we don't hurry.'

'Yes, you're right. Sorry.'

He was already on the bank, towelling his long brown body vigorously and rubbing his hair into a dark wayward tangle. Paul was stripping now, to reveal a brief navy swimming costume. He took Janet's towel from her and started rubbing her down, then planted kisses on her face and shoulders in a possessive way which she found irritating, especially in front of other people.

'You've got your beeper, Paul?' Clifford said, half-dressed now in cool cream canvas jeans that emphasised the tan of his lean muscular torso.

'Of course.'

'Just checking,' Clifford smiled thinly.

'You didn't need to.'

Clifford ignored Paul's low growled reply and turned to Janet.

'And Janet. That hair . . . If you're called out too, you won't want it wet. May I suggest you let it out for a while so it will dry quicker? Anyway, have a nice night.'

'You too,' Paul said coldly. Janet was too angry to reply at all.

Marcia murmured a good night too, and took Clifford's bare arm. They climbed the bank together. Clifford had his olive-green shirt slung carelessly over one shoulder, obviously intending to put it on later, and in spite of her anger, Janet could not help being aware of him as a man in the casual dress and pose which suited him so well.

She blocked the dangerous thought firmly, reminding herself of how awkward she felt with him most of the time and how unfairly judgemental he was about herself and Paul. She didn't need to remind herself about the way he kept harping on about her hair. So much for her idea that swimming with him might form some slight level of common ground between them!

'Coming back in the water with me?' Paul said.

'For a minute,' Janet replied.

But she did not really enjoy it. Paul didn't seem to want to swim, and just used the water as an excuse to go on holding her, entangling his wet limbs with hers and standing where they were only chest deep. Janet's head was heavy with water after her playful swim with Clifford, and she would have preferred to sit on the bank for a while, soaking up the last of the sun before they began the picnic meal.

Paul talked all through the simple meal of bread, salad and cold meat, and that was irritating too. Janet liked to observe and listen when she was in the bush, and sunset was such an interesting and beautiful time. With constant talk, they would scare away any animals who might have come down to the water at this spot for their evening drink.

Paul had promised to bring insect repellent but had forgotten, so that what with eating, making light replies to his repartee, and slapping at mosquitoes, Janet could not enjoy the evening sights and sounds at all. She really wasn't feeling very romantic when he reached across and drew her towards him for a kiss after the remnants of the meal were packed away, and the touch of his lips aroused no response in her.

'What's the matter?' he asked after a moment.

'I'm being bitten alive.'

'Oh.'

'Sorry, but honestly, aren't you?' Janet said. She knew she was pouring cold water on his mood, but she just couldn't enjoy herself like this. Somehow, the sour end to her swim with Clifford had a lot to do with her mood, too, though she tried not to keep thinking about it.

'They don't seem to like the taste of me much for some reason,' Paul said. 'I suppose you'd like to leave?'

'If you don't mind . . .'

'Well, I do, but I understand.'

The silence as they gathered up rug, towels, wet costumes and picnic things was not a relaxed one, but Janet didn't know how to redeem the situation. She was simply suspecting more and more that she and Paul just didn't have much in common and that their time in Sydney had been something brief and fleeting that was best forgotten about, if only Paul could see it the same way.

He slowed outside Lorna Hammond's roadhouse fifteen minutes later.

'Shall I drop you off?' he asked. 'Or shall we head back to the hotel, or to my place to listen to some records? There's nothing else on tonight in this god-forsaken town.'

'If you feel like that about Benanda, why do you stay?' Janet said reasonably.

'I'm beginning to wonder.'

CHAPTER FIVE

THE rift that had opened between Janet and Paul that night did not close, and it left Janet a little more lonely in the town than she had expected to be. Not that she really blamed Paul. They had both had expectations of a closer relationship after getting on so well in Sydney, but with hindsight, Janet could see that those expectations had been founded on very shaky ground. She had been too flattered by his attention, and he had seen her as livelier and more flirtatious than she really was. They still met for an occasional drink, and got on well enough when working together, but were just too unalike to be able to form a solid friendship, let alone fall in love. Janet did not think that he was really hurt, remembering what Susan Adams had said about him being a 'confirmed bachelor', but she knew he was piqued.

The coolness between herself and Paul did not bring Janet any closer to Clifford Ransome, however. She knew he had noticed that she wasn't spending very much time with Paul, and that he was pleased about it. This annoyed her very much. What did the man expect her to be? A nun, or something! Devoted body and soul to her nursing. It was ridiculous. Especially since Clifford himself spent so much time out at Fairwater Park with Marcia.

Janet would not admit to herself that there was another reason for her dislike of Clifford Ransome, and for her faint general depression, but there was. It might have seemed a stupid reason to most people, but it wasn't to Janet.

Her hair . . . Washing it in harsh, mineral-filled bore water, trying to dry it quickly after swimming in the river, keeping it free of dust and tangles in the hot summer winds, and making sure that it never, never fell down from its high twisted knot while she was on duty with Clifford Ransome.

Inevitably, she was coming to admit that the senior doctor's first blunt statement to her about it had been right: It would have to come off.

But not yet. Lorna would offer to do it, but Janet didn't really want to entrust such a task to her. She would have to arrange to get to a good hairdresser in Broken Hill somehow. And the longer she left it, the less it would look like a capitulation to Clifford Ransome's orders.

He had said nothing about it since that time at the river, seeming very much absorbed in his own life and not altogether happy about some private concern, but she suspected that he was just waiting till she settled in properly before insisting that she do something about it.

These thoughts were revolving unproductively in Janet's head after she had just washed her hair one Sunday morning three weeks after her arrival at Benanda. She was on call, but somehow felt that a hot Sunday morning was not a very likely time for an emergency. If she stood in the sun to dry, she would soon be able to tuck it away in coiled plaits and get on with a day of helping Lorna to make apricot jam.

It was the kind of task she liked. Lorna bought big boxes of the fruit from the Murray River irrigation area near Mildura, where her son lived, and made great batches of jams and preserved fruit, selling them to townspeople and to passers-by in her roadhouse. Janet received a reduction in rent in return for the assistance she gave, but did not do it for the money. She simply enjoyed the sense of satisfaction that came from surveying the rows of jams and bottles at the end of hours of slicing, stirring and ladling.

Janet knew that Lorna planned to start work in half an hour, so she stood outside and combed energetically in the hot morning sun.

The phone in her flat rang before she had got half-way through the task, and her heart sank. It was an ominous sound at this time of day. Clifford's voice, brisk and business-like, came through the line.

'Janet?'

'Yes, speaking.'

'You're needed, I'm afraid. The call's just come through. Beth Pooley up on Coolingee station is in labour. I'll come and get you, but I've got another radio call that could be important . . .'

'I can ride over,' Janet said quickly. 'Lorna has lent me a bike. It'll be quicker that way.'

'Good girl. See you soon.'

He hung up without a wasted word, and only then did Janet remember her hair, still a knotted mess on one side and very wet. She felt almost ill for a moment. It would take at least ten minutes to fix properly, and Clifford would be rightly impatient at the delay. But perhaps if she hurried and ignored the tangles . . .

Five minutes later it was in two rough, ugly plaits which she twisted hastily on to the top of her head be-fore changing into her uniform and hurrying across to Lorna's kitchen to say that she would not be able to help with the jam-making after all.

Then she was off on the bike, still a bit wobbly as it was the kind with a cross-bar and low-pitched handle-bars and she wasn't used to it. Her hair was still very damp and there were frequent puffs of wind which would blow up dust, but that wasn't important. She just had to get to the Base before Clifford started to get angry.

Janet was so keyed up to this goal that she didn't look out for traffic as carefully as she normally would have done. In any case, she was becoming very used to Benanda's quiet streets after the hellish bustle of Syd-ney. The big road-train—a great prime-mover with three empty cattle-trucks coupled to it—took her com-pletely by surprise as it thundered up behind her on the narrow bitumen strip of Benanda's main street, blaring its horn at her and forcing her off on to the red dirt of the verge.

The road-train was so wide and cumbersome that the wheels of the cattle-truck at the end slipped onto the dirt quite often too, churning up thick dust. Janet panicked at the noise, at the sudden change of her course, and at the reduced visibility through the dust and did not see the pothole in front of her wheel.

A moment later, she was on the ground, the wheels of the bike still spinning crazily on top of her. She had given her head a bit of a bump, and had a slight graze on one arm but was otherwise unhurt, but this minor accident could not be allowed to get in the way of her emergency flight to Coolingee.

'I'm not going to be silly,' she told herself firmly, blinking back tears of shock, and standing up straight to brush herself down. She took a deep breath or two, then examined the bike. It was undamaged, fortunately. The truck was already nearly out of sight, and its driver either had not seen her fall, or had not cared.

Her dress was brushed comparatively clean and the graze on her arm had not even properly broken the skin. The whole incident was very minor, and was now over. Janet picked up the bike and rode off again—more slowly because the experience had rattled her, but otherwise admirably in control.

Clifford Ransome was pacing impatiently on the verandah of the Base building when Janet skidded to a halt outside a few minutes later. She was about to give a quick explanation of what had happened as she climbed the two steps to reach him, but he spoke before she could do so.

'Janet, your hair looks absolutely terrible.' His tone was blunt, clipped and angry.

'Oh, yes, I had to do it up in a hurry, and then . . .'

'It's more than that. Haven't you felt it, or looked at it? What happened?'

He pulled her inside and marched her to a mirror in

the toilet area as if she were a school-girl who had flouted uniform regulations. Janet was appalled at what she saw in the bright fluorescent-lit mirror. Thick red dust must have caked onto her still-wet hair when she hit the ground after her fall, and one of her plaits, braided more loosely than usual in her haste, hung down slackly in its twisted coil.

Muddy strands of hair had brushed against her face, leaving red streaks which she had not felt in her slight shock after the fall from the bike. She put up a hand that was almost trembling and felt the heavy plaited coils. They were already stiffening with dried mud. Clifford still stood accusingly behind her and their eyes met in the reflection from the mirror.

'I washed it,' she said clumsily. 'It was still wet when you rang. Then I fell from the bike and it got covered in dust.'

'You'll have to put something over it. Have you got a scarf?'

'No.'

'You can't possibly go and deliver a baby like that.'

'I'm sorry.'

She waited for him to positively order her to chop her hair off then and there, but he said nothing for a moment, only continued to stare at her reflection with a mixture of accusation and . . . but she could not define the other emotion she saw in his face.

'I'll get some gauze bandage and we'll make some kind of turban.'

He was gone before she could reply, leaving the swing door of the bathroom to bump back and forth violently with a harsh squeak. Quickly, Janet neatened the stiff plaits as much as she could and wiped the streaks from her face then left the bathroom, meeting Clifford just outside the door.

With skilled, economical movements, as if he bandaged up recalcitrant piles of hair every day, he folded the square of gauze into a tight turban that concealed every dusty strand, and produced white surgical tape to fasten the odd-looking parcel.

'You look as though you've got head injuries,' he said. 'Goodness knows what they'll think of you at Coolingee, but it can't be helped. We've got to get going.'

He was already moving towards the door that led in the direction of the waiting plane. Janet followed, hot with mixed emotions. Clifford could have been much angrier—but perhaps he was saving it for later. He was striding rapidly, his shoulders tense. He wore khaki pants and an immaculately white shirt, its sleeves rolled above the elbows. He looked completely competent and Janet felt like a slattern by contrast.

If only he hadn't aroused her antagonism in the very beginning, she might not have rebelled against him and this might not be happening. But no, her own stubbornness wasn't an excuse. She felt utterly miserable.

They had almost reached the plane when he turned to her, and she steeled herself for his anger, staring at the horizon because she simply couldn't bear to meet it face to face, remembering how his shoulders set square and his forehead creased deeply . . .

'Listen . . . I might not get another chance to say this.' To her great surprise, his tone was quite gentle. 'You'll probably have to work hard today, and I won't be able to be there. Bill's dropping you off at Coolingee then flying on further north with me. An accident I've got to see to. Take the day off tomorrow, and Tuesday.'

'Thank you, but it doesn't matter . . .' She dared to look at him now, and he met her gaze steadily with his dark brown eyes. Suddenly she was extra keen to prove her professionalism to him. 'I don't want time off.'

'You'll need it.' He paused for a moment, then continued. 'Constable Connolly is driving in to Broken Hill tomorrow to collect his wife. She has been staying with her sister there. They'll be coming back on Tuesday. If you wanted a trip into town . . . for any reason, I'm sure they'd be happy to take you.'

They had reached the plane and he gave her no chance to reply before jumping up into the front passenger seat of the Piper Chieftain. Janet took her own accustomed place in the back, feeling an absurd desire to cry. Clifford Ransome was actually respecting the stubbornness she was now becoming ashamed of and letting her make her own decision. All he had done to persuade her was to offer her a way of getting to Broken Hill—which meant she could go to a hairdresser and not have to submit to Lorna's well-meant but probably less-than-skilled barbering techniques.

And when she had expected only an unleashing of his anger! He was . . . Oh, she didn't understand him, didn't even think that she liked him most of the time, but he was certainly a surprising man.

Less than an hour later, the plane touched down at Coolingee's modest airstrip. Glenn Pooley almost ran across to it from his waiting vehicle, and virtually snatched the bag of equipment Janet was carrying. He was clearly too worried about his wife to take any notice of Janet's weird head-gear, and Janet herself had almost forgotten it by this time.

'You've taken longer than I expected,' he said, his voice tight with anxiety.

'Is she all right?' Clifford said, opening the door of the plane. They had been in radio contact with the homestead for the first part of the journey, but then had had to tune in to another call.

'Yes, she's fine . . . At least, the same as last time, she says.'

'Off you go, then Janet. We can't wait,' Clifford said. Bill Kirkley was already revving the engines ready to turn again for the take-off.

Mrs Pooley was in the spare-room of the homestead, which had been specially fitted out for use as a delivery room according to directions Paul Adams had given on last month's clinic visit. It was Mrs Pooley's second pregnancy, and the first had gone so smoothly in the hospital at Broken Hill that she was keen to have this one in the familiar surroundings of her own home.

She was pacing about now, quite cheerful between the contractions which seized her every five minutes or so, and after making a cervical examination, Janet could tell by its dilation that the birth was still several hours off.

'Don't hang round, Glenn,' Beth Pooley said. 'Now that Sister Green is here, I feel quite safe. We'll make some tea and you go and get on with fixing the pump.'

'Love . . .'

'Go on! Sister Green will call you when I need you.'

After this, time became a disjointed thing, measured in the minutes between contractions and the seconds of the pain's duration. Beth Pooley squatted, paced and groaned. Janet vaguely heard sounds coming from the kitchen as Glenn Pooley distractedly fixed himself a rough lunch. His wife was now in too much pain to feel hunger, and Janet was too busy.

At two o'clock she went in search of Mr Pooley and found him on the shaded verandah, riffling back and forth through an agricultural magazine.

'You'd better come in now, if you want to help your wife through the final stage and see the birth,' she said, and he jumped up immediately, turning pale.

Beth Pooley was red and damp with effort now, but managed a smile when she saw her husband.

'I'd forgotten that it was all such . . . damn . . . hard . . . work,' she said, finishing with a long groan.

Half an hour later it was all over, and David John Pooley, a healthy eight-pound boy, had made a safe entry into the world.

'A son! I'm tickled, I can tell you!' Glenn Pooley said. 'A brother and sister we've got now. Jackie's over at her grandmother's at Kilalpanundra. We sent her a week ago to stay till it was all over. Wait till she hears!'

Janet was full of congratulations, but then she had more work to do, examining the baby thoroughly to check that he was as healthy as he seemed, and making Mrs Pooley comfortable after her hours of hard work and pain so that she could fall asleep. Paul Adams would pay a visit to Coolingee tomorrow, but Janet had to make sure that everything would be all right till then.

It was late afternoon when she radioed Benanda Base to say that she was ready to be picked up.

'Bill will get you,' Martin Baird, the radio operator at the Base, informed her.

'Will Dr Ransome be with him?' Janet asked. Surprisingly, she found she was hoping he would be.

'I shouldn't think so,' Martin replied cheerfully. 'He's home again. Fixed up the accident at Terangie Bore. A crushed foot, it was, but the guy's going to be fine.'

'Oh, thanks. I'll wait for Bill then. Over and out.'

Janet suppressed a shudder. A crushed foot! And her wretched hair had delayed the flight by many vital minutes. It had become more than a personal friction between herself and Dr Ransome now. This time the patient had not suffered, but another time it might have been different. She was definitely going to Broken Hill tomorrow. Over two hundred miles for a haircut! It brought home to her once again just how frighteningly desolate and unpopulated this region was.

Janet rang Constable Connolly first thing on arriving back home and he agreed to pick her up at eight the next morning, saying that he wanted to leave reasonably early as it was over five hours' drive.

The journey into Broken Hill was a hot one, as, with the imminent approach of Christmas, summer was well and truly upon them. Bob Connolly was an entertaining driving companion, however, being full of stories about the region and about incidents he had stumbled across during his eight years as Benanda's only policeman.

'So you'd like to go to a hairdresser?' he asked her as they neared the town just before two. 'There's a nice place near my wife's sister's. Young-looking styles on the posters in the windows, if I'm any judge. I'll drop you there. Where are you staying tonight?'

'I thought a hotel . . .'

'Glenys will have you—that's Iris's sister.'

'Oh, I couldn't impose . . .'

But he insisted, with the open hospitality of country people, and Janet agreed in the end. He had been right about the hairdresser, too. A friendly, fashion-conscious young woman came up to Janet when she entered the bright-mirrored salon, and she looked quite excited at the chance of doing something very stylish on someone who was pretty and well-dressed.

'You want it all off?' she asked sympathetically. Janet nodded.

'Yes, please. It's just too difficult in this climate.'

'Yes, it would be. You'd like to keep the plait as a souvenir though?'

'If I could.'

'No problem. And I'll do one of those new bob styles, very short at the back. It'll really suit you if you'd like that?'

'Yes. It'll be cool . . .' Janet could not quite bring herself to think that it might look nice as well.

The whole thing was accomplished very quickly, and a completely new face stared back at her from the big mirror, framed in fluffy hair that had sprung up and bounced out, full of body and life now that it was not weighed down by its length.

'Your head's just the right shape for it, and you're so petite. It looks great,' the hairdresser enthused, but Janet couldn't agree—yet. The change was too great. She fled, not staying to buy shampoo or conditioning mousse, or styling gel, or anything else that the girl wanted to sell her. She skulked for an hour in a café —one without mirrors—before finding Constable Connolly's sister-in-law's house nearby.

She spent a pleasant night with the Connollys and their relations and enjoyed the chance of getting to know

Iris Connolly, who turned out to be a friendly down-to-earth woman in her late twenties. She had only been married to Bob for two years, but seemed to enjoy the quiet life at Benanda and not to miss the comparative bustle of Broken Hill very much.

She was keen to hear all Bob's news during the journey back, and was curious about every car that passed, waving to familiar faces and speculating about the possible identity of unfamiliar ones. It was in the second half of the journey that they overtook a new-looking Toyota four-wheel-drive which was parked in some shade while its occupants had a snack.

'Who was that, Bob?' dark-haired Iris Connolly asked, turning her head to look back.

'Who was it! Don't you recognise Kevin Fairfax's Toyota?'

'Oh yes, of course, but I mean who was with him? It certainly wasn't Gloria. Or Marcia.'

'Couldn't tell you then. But they're bound to overtake us when they get going again, the way Kevin drives. You can get another look then, love.' Bob Connolly chuckled at his wife's country-style curiosity.

Ten minutes later the vehicle did come up behind them and gave a friendly toot before overtaking. Iris turned and waved, studying the woman in the passenger seat keenly.

'I reckon it's Stephanie Beddie!' she exclaimed.

'Whew! Didn't think she'd be back up here,' Bob Connolly said. 'Not this soon, anyway.'

'Did Frank say anything about it on the transceiver?'

'Not that I heard. And no one's mentioned it. They must be trying to keep it quiet till they see how she settles in.'

'I suppose Frank'll be picking her up in Benanda this afternoon,' Iris speculated. 'Unless it's not him she's come back for at all, but . . .'

'Hang on! That's just a rumour, isn't it? What about Marcia?'

'Who knows . . .'

Janet said nothing during all this, though there were many questions she would have liked to ask. It seemed that the whole of the outback community was interested in Frank and Stephanie Beddie, and clearly her absence from Diri Diri was not simply because she was taking a holiday down south. As for that last comment, weighted with significance as it had been—what was she to make of that?

An hour later they arrived at Benanda, and Janet was dropped off at Lorna's after willingly promising to visit Iris Connolly at her home for afternoon tea soon.

'There's a message for you from the Base, love,' Mrs Hammond called to Janet from beside a car which she was filling with petrol. Janet came over at once.

'Urgent? I'm not on call . . .'

'No, nothing urgent,' Lorna reassured her. 'Your hair looks lovely, dear, by the way. I think you did the right thing. Are you happy with it?'

'Not yet,' Janet admitted. 'My head still feels as light as air, and I just can't get used to it.'

'But you will.'

'I know,' Janet nodded. 'Ask me about it again in a week's time.'

'Anyway, the message was that you're to go over to the Base this afternoon if you can. Paul needs to discuss a few things about Beth Pooley and her baby with you. Just routine, apparently.'

'I'll ride over on the bike,' Janet said. 'My legs need a stretch after that drive.'

'Would you be able to take something over there for me?' Lorna asked now.

'Of course.'

'I promised Dr Ransome some jam from this batch. If it's too heavy to carry on the bike I can easily run it over myself some other time though.'

'No, I'll take it.'

Janet spent twenty minutes in her room, taking a quick cold shower, flicking through her strange-feeling new hairstyle with a brush and changing from her aqua cotton sun-dress into a white T-shirt with a big hand-water-coloured peony on the front that matched the fashionably baggy salmon-coloured shorts she teamed with it. Simple leather sandals—cool and practical for bike-riding—and a wide-brimmed pale straw sun-hat completed the outfit.

Lorna loaded the front carrier-basket with four pots of jam, then Janet was on her way. Dr Ransome was on a flight when she arrived at the Base, but Paul was there and he actually didn't recognise her at first in the sun-glasses and hat and with the new chopped and bouncy hairstyle framing her face.

'Janet!' he exclaimed at last.

'Yes, it's me,' she said meekly.

'It looks good. Spur of the moment idea, was it?'

'Not exactly,' Janet said. There was no point in trying to explain to Paul. Fleetingly, the thought flashed through her mind that, in spite of his initial anger, Clifford Ransome had seemed in the end to understand at least a part of what she was feeling without needing explanations.

'Clifford's out on a flight. Is it serious?' she heard herself ask. The image of him at work—quick, capable, completely involved—rose in her mind's eye.

'Possibly. It's someone we're thinking of bringing in here for monitoring,' Paul explained.

Benanda Base was actually equipped with five hospital beds and quite a variety of equipment which could be used to care for patients who were too ill to be treated at home, but whose condition did not warrant their being taken to the city or to Broken Hill. Since Janet's arrival, only two of the beds had been used, but Clifford had said that in the next few years they hoped to expand the hospital facilities at the Base, which made more sense than having to make the trip to Broken Hill so often, especially with the growth of the gasfields in the area.

Janet and Paul spent an hour going through various aspects of Beth Pooley's case, as well as those of some of the other patients who had received emergency treatment lately, then the distinctive sound of the Piper Chieftain's engine was heard overhead and a few minutes later Clifford entered.

'Did you bring Mrs Robins in?' Paul asked.

'No, I decided there was no need in the end. It's best for her morale if she's treated at home, and I'll keep in radio contact every day.'

While he was speaking, Janet slipped out of the room. She did not know why she felt unable to face him with her radical change in appearance. She would have to sooner or later, after all. But not yet. She took refuge in the bathroom for a while, studying herself in the mirror again and trying to find the reflexion she felt comfortable with somewhere in the new jaunty look.

When she emerged, she could no longer hear voices in the Base office, and presumed Clifford had left. Perhaps she could just go home. But no, she had better check that Paul had finished talking with her.

But it was Clifford, not Paul who was in the office.

He sat at his desk writing, a frown creasing his brow, but turned when Janet entered. For a long moment they simply stared at each other, saying nothing, but sharing a complex series of emotions without words.

Of course he took in her bobbed head at a glance, and his half-smile communicated approval, regret, admiration and sympathy all at once. It was Janet who finally had to break the silence.

'I've had it chopped.' She was deliberately flippant.

'So I see.'

'I feel . . . a bit lost.'

'Janet!'

Effortlessly, she was in his arms, giving way to tears which she knew were foolish but could not suppress. She had to mourn her loss fully this one time, and somehow,

Clifford was the right person to seek refuge with. He seemed to understand what she was feeling and cradled her like a child, kissing the top of her head and holding her in a strong grasp.

'Oh dear, silly me,' she laughed, her voice sounding cloggy from the tears. She lifted her head from his shoulder and saw that she had left a damp patch there, a darker colour in the soft fabric of his shirt. She should pull away, she knew, but didn't want to. His arms felt very firm and safe.

'Not silly,' he said softly. 'Will it help if I say you look even more lovely now?'

'A bit. Even if it's not true,' she said softly back.

Their gazes locked. His warm brown eyes, with the slightly bruised expression that she could never fathom, were only inches from her own as he bent over her. For a long moment they stayed like this, then he kissed her, his lips gentle and exploring and sweet.

Janet melted against him, not questioning her own feelings or his, not remembering that she usually felt awkward in his company. She wanted this to go on for a long time . . .

Clifford was the one to let go his hold, finding it hard to stay in control and suddenly questioning the whole thing. This was his nurse. This was the young woman who had come up here because of an affair with Paul, and Clifford himself had felt very harsh about that. What did he mean by this kiss? What was he feeling? Under the immediate physical effect of it, he just didn't know. And it wasn't only his feelings for Janet that had been called into question when he had given way to his impulse . . .

'I'm sorry,' he said, steeling himself to be cool now, although didn't even know quite what he was afraid of betraying to her.

'I've got some jam for you . . . from Lorna,' Janet said, far too quickly. 'You ordered it, she said. But I've left it outside in the basket of my bike. I'll get it.'

She had retreated from him, embarrassed and confused at her response. This kiss had nearly happened that first night at Glencoe Downs. Then she had blamed a drink and moonlight, and the special quality of the outback summer night, but here in the tepid air of the Base office on a hot afternoon . . . What was going on?

'Yes, the jam,' he was saying. 'Look, let's forget about this whole thing, shall we?'

'If you want . . . I mean, yes,' she finished firmly, feeling a strange disappointment fighting against her rational mind.

It was a brief kiss. A physical impulse. It meant nothing. Of course they should forget it. Why had he even felt the need to say something? He was involved with Marcia Fairfax—wasn't he? As for herself, perhaps she was still just a bit lonely here in Benanda. That was all it had been—the need for some human reassurance.

Paul came out of the radio room.

'I wouldn't mind a bit of a break. Can you take over, Cliff?'

'Of course,' the senior doctor replied, too quickly.

'I'll leave the jam on your desk,' Janet put in.

She slipped out onto the verandah. There was a chair in the shade at the far end, half-hidden from the rest of the verandah by a wooden lattice screen where someone —Clifford, perhaps—was valiantly attempting to grow a creeper. Janet decided just to sit there for a while and go back inside with the jam later on. Clifford wouldn't be waiting for it. He probably wouldn't even notice her delay since he was in the radio room. His kiss had left her weak and drained of emotion and she needed this moment of solitude.

A Toyota four-wheel drive pulled up outside the Base only a short while later. Janet recognised its occupants as Kevin Fairfax and his companion—Stephanie Beddie, if Iris Connolly had been right. They unloaded several hefty pieces of luggage from the back of the vehicle, while speaking.

'Are you sure this will be all right, Stephanie?' Kevin Fairfax asked.

'Perfectly sure. Frank arranged to pick me up here. He said he'd try to get in around four, and it must be just about that. I don't mind waiting around for him anyway. There are . . . one or two people I'd like to catch up with.'

'Well, if you're sure . . .'

'I am,' she assured him. 'And thanks again for the lift up. It was so convenient that you happened to be making the trip. Thank Gloria for me, too, won't you, for that late lunch?'

'Sure. Of course.'

'I'll be seeing you whenever, then.'

'Good to have you back in the area.' Kevin Fairfax said it cheerfully, but Janet thought she detected a slightly forced note.

He drove off. Stephanie Beddie turned and surveyed the Base building, a strange expression on her face before stepping up on to the verandah. She was quite a tall woman, but very slender and willowy, with ash blonde hair and a pale, almost transparent complexion. She was pretty, but it was the kind of prettiness that can easily fade into a weak, washed-out look if circumstances are not happy. And Stephanie Beddie did not look completely happy. Even with her restricted view through the lattice, Janet could see that.

She did not seem to have noticed Janet sitting quietly in her half-hidden corner, and was about to open the screen-door when it swung outwards and Clifford Ransome stepped through.

'Clifford!'

'I heard your voice.'

'I was crossing my fingers you'd be here and not on a flight,' Stephanie Beddie said, a little breathlessly. 'That's why I asked Frank to pick me up here.'

'Frank's just radioed in, actually,' Clifford replied, giving her a stiff hug but then pushing away the arms she still held out to him. Janet's hands tightened on the arm of her wicker chair as she saw the movement. If Clifford had not been in the arms of another woman—herself!—not ten minutes before, she was sure that his embrace would have been much warmer.

'Radioed in!' Stephanie was saying blankly. 'Oh no! That means . . .'

'Yes. He's had a breakdown. Some problem in the vehicle's transmission. He was only about twenty miles from Coonalamine Downs, fortunately, so they'll put him up there and should manage to fix the car by tomorrow.'

'I'll have to stay in town then,' Stephanie said.

'I'm afraid so.' Clifford's tone was unreadable.

'Could I . . . stay with you?' She tilted her head to one side and smiled up at him uncertainly, but he answered quickly and shortly.

'No, Stephanie, that's impossible.'

'Why?'

'You know perfectly well why.' His voice was harsh and Janet could hear the tension of repressed feelings built up inside him.

She wished she could escape from her position as unwilling eavesdropper but she would either have had to walk directly past them, or climb the railing that fronted the verandah. Quickly, she took a book from the leather bag she had brought with her and pretended to read. She wasn't trying to hide. If they had looked, they would have seen her, even behind the lattice screen. In a moment, with any luck, they would go inside.

They didn't, though.

'You'll have to stay in the hotel,' Clifford was saying now.

'The hotel! I couldn't!'

'I don't see that there's any choice.'

'But . . . Please, Clifford!' It was a beseeching wail.

'Stephanie, why must you make things so hard?'

Clifford had lowered his voice now. Before he had been speaking quite loudly, as if stressing that theirs was a public conversation for anyone to hear, but now it was clearly intended to be private.

'What are you asking from me?' he continued, rasping out the words. 'You've come back here to be with Frank—haven't you?'

'I don't know. I don't know.' Stephanie was nearly crying now. 'Of course I thought that by coming back, Frank and I . . . But seeing you . . . and I haven't even got home or seen Frank yet and already I feel . . .' She could not go on.

'I'm going to ring the hotel.' Clifford broke in to try to control her with a calm tone and a restraining arm on her shoulder.

'Yes, all right,' she nodded, recovered somewhat now. 'If only Kevin hadn't left. I could have stayed out at Fairwater with him and Gloria. That would have been bearable. It's so beautiful out there, and not a hundred miles from nowhere like Diri Diri.' She suppressed a shudder.

'I will not let you speak like that!' Clifford was immediately angry again. 'You're not even giving things a chance. I thought we'd agreed . . . Look, I'm going to ring the hotel now, and then I'll let Frank know that you're here.'

He turned on his heel and went inside, leaving the woman to stare helplessly at her pile of luggage for a moment before following him. Janet waited for a few moments then went inside too, slipping quietly through the door, Lorna's jam in one hand.

Clifford had just hung up and was turning away from the phone when she entered. For a moment their gaze locked across the room—hers confused and apprehensive, his hunted and distant—then he was looking at Stephanie Beddie.

'The hotel is full. A team of geologists on their way down from the new mining exploration area. I imagine they're going home for Christmas. You've picked a bad time of year to arrive.'

Janet could see that he was using the uncharacteristically long explanation to conceal the tension in the air from Paul, who was only now getting around to making the coffee from the water Janet had boiled. Stephanie glanced at Paul before she replied, using a bright, casual tone.

'Never mind,' she said. 'We'll just have to go back to your original plan. I'll have to stay with you.'

Janet saw Clifford's jaw tighten, but what could he say? Stephanie had been very audacious, taking a wicked advantage of Paul's presence, and Janet's own, as neutral parties.

'Yes, very well then,' Clifford said tightly, then turned to Paul. 'Lance is around, isn't he?'

'Think so.'

'I'll get him to help with your luggage, Stephanie. By the way, I don't suppose you've met Sister Green.'

He introduced the two women briefly, then strode towards the door. Stephanie smiled vaguely at Janet and Paul, and followed him out of the room.

'Coffee?' Paul asked laconically. Surely he must have noticed the tension? Perhaps he simply didn't care.

'No thanks,' Janet said. 'I've got to go. I only came back because . . . I'd forgotten this jam from Lorna for Clifford.'

She had become suddenly and horribly aware that in contrast to Paul, she cared too much. Paul tossed her a casual farewell and she responded absently, then got herself away.

Stephanie Beddie was going to spend the night with Clifford, and from the way they had talked to each other it was clear that they were lovers—or they had been, and Stephanie, at least, was determined that it would continue. Stephanie had been quite open about it, and Clifford had undoubtedly only hesitated out of a desire to maintain appearances.

It seemed clear, now, to Janet, where Marcia Fairfax came into the picture, too. She and Clifford didn't really have much in common. He was simply using her as a blind, but no one was really fooled, if Bob and Iris Connolly's comments in the car this afternoon had been any indication. Apparently, even Frank Beddie himself had some idea of what was going on. Janet had not imagined the crackling tension in the air and the wariness between the two men the afternoon they had visited Diri Diri.

But why did she find this new knowledge so appalling? It wasn't just that her own private nature would have shrunk from the idea of such a complicated and public triangle. It was a more personal and hurtful reason than that.

'I'm not falling in love with him,' she whispered helplessly as she wheeled Lorna's old bike out into the road. 'I can't be. Especially not now. I ought to despise him.'

That was why it hurt. To think that she had unknowingly been forming an attraction to him, that she had responded so strongly to his kiss, and to find that he had not one but two less than honourable liaisons already!

CHAPTER SIX

CHRISTMAS passed in a blanket of heat. Janet spent it quietly, sharing the incongruous but traditional hot midday meal with Lorna and her son and his family, who had made the long drive up from Mildura to be with her for a few days and help her with some work around the service station. Afterwards, Lorna would close the road-house for two weeks and get in a local lad to keep the petrol bowsers running when required, while she returned with her son to Mildura for a holiday there on the wide banks of the River Murray. Janet found it enjoyable to be part of a family for a change, and did not mind the antics of Lorna's two excited grandchildren.

That evening, she had a meal of cold turkey, ham and salad—much better suited to the climate—at Bob and Iris Connolly's small house adjoining the police station.

It had been a surprise invitation, but a very welcome one, and Janet enjoyed meeting Pat Jackson, a softly-spoken man in his mid-twenties who was taking over the management of his parents' property about forty miles from Benanda. Janet suspected that he had been invited especially for her own benefit, as he was both present-able, and unattached, and Iris was one of the region's most ardent match-makers.

Before the evening was over, Pat had invited her out to look over the property, and she had promised to contact him about the idea when next she had time off. Iris was clearly disappointed that things had not moved a little faster, but Janet, as always, felt uncomfortable about having other people keep an eye on the developments of any relationship in her life.

It was less than a week since Stephanie Beddie had passed through Benanda, and the whole thing was still

very much in Janet's mind. She had been wakened early
by an emergency call the morning after Stephanie's night
at Clifford's, and on arriving at the Base, had found that
she was to make the flight with Paul.

It was the first time she had been teamed with him,
and of course that was significant. Clifford was with
Stephanie and did not want to be disturbed.

As sometimes happened, panic at their distance from
help had led the emergency callers to exaggerate the
seriousness of the road accident, and Paul and Janet
arrived back at Benanda quite early, without having to
bring any patients back for treatment. Janet could not
help taking a long look at the doctor's nearby house.
Stephanie Beddie was there on the screened verandah at
the side of the house, lingering over breakfast in a pale
lacy night-gown. Clifford wasn't beside her, but that
could mean anything. Probably he was simply in the
kitchen making more coffee.

As for Clifford's unexpected kiss, it was incredible
how quickly that receded into the past as the days went
by. It all seemed quite unreal now. The senior doctor
was very distant, very pre-occupied, very business-like,
whenever she saw him at the Base now. He had made no
further comment about her hair, and she felt—probably
foolishly—that he had let her down. At one time, he had
seemed to understand.

He had sent her on a second flight with Paul, too.

'He's obviously stopped caring whether we're involved together or not,' Janet thought. 'Either that, or
he'd rather risk us conducting an affair during working
hours, or whatever it is he was afraid of before, than
spend time with me himself.'

She told herself that she didn't care a bit if there was
yet another reason for awkwardness between them, but
that wasn't true. There had been moments in the month
she had known him when they had seemed to be groping
towards a friendship, and that might have been nice.
Now, he virtually ignored her, and when their eyes did

meet, Janet could see a veiled awareness in him—the embarrassed memory of that misguided kiss.

She had known a kiss to wreck a friendship before now. In fact, from shared confidences with nursing friends, she suspected it to be a common enough thing. Two people who barely knew each other and had little in common, a brief moment of proximity and physical awareness, and then an awkwardness which never fully disappeared. Avoiding each other was really the best thing.

Clifford seemed to have reached the same conclusion. He spent both Christmas and New Year celebrating at Fairwater Park, and Marcia was seen even more often in his company now, as if he wanted to make sure that there was no gossip about himself and Stephanie. Janet wondered what was happening out at Diri Diri now that Stephanie was back with Frank. Did she have any contact with Clifford? If they did, it could only be by radio or letter. The whole thing was weird, and what was Marcia Fairfax's attitude to it all? Did she think he was using her?

The girl did not seem any more content with life in Benanda. Why didn't she leave the town and live in the city instead? Presumably it was Clifford that kept her here, whatever the strange nature of their relationship.

Early in January, it was time for another clinic flight, this time to the north-east. John Hunt, the dentist, and his nurse Jill Wilkinson, would take part in it, too, and Dr Ransome announced that Paul would go while he would stay behind at Benanda to handle emergency work in the other plane, flown by their second pilot, Lance Norton.

Janet was waiting beside Air Doctor One just before half-past seven on the Monday morning of the flight. John Hunt and Jill Wilkinson were already there. They had been flown up from Broken Hill the previous afternoon when Bill had gone down there to collect some supplies, and had spent the night at the hotel.

Jill was a pleasant-faced and plumpish blonde of about Janet's own age, and John was an older, grey-haired man with a gentle, worried-looking face, as though he had looked into a few too many unhealthy mouths in his lifetime. Bill made introductions, but there was still no sign of Paul.

The heat of the day was building up, and Janet was not surprised at what John Hunt said as they waited.

'Forecast last night said we were in for a scorcher,' he said. 'Low forties. That's nearly 110 on the old scale.'

'And there are still two more months of summer!' Jill said with a groan.

'We've got the river running deep though, this year, after the good season in the east,' Bill said. 'I try and get out there nearly every day. It makes a difference.'

Paul was late now, and Janet was surprised. She knew that he was a casual sort of person about many things, but he did take his work seriously. Then to her surprise she saw Clifford coming briskly across from his house, his long legs making big strides without apparent effort.

'Paul rang twenty minutes ago,' he said when he reached them. 'He's developed a cold overnight, ludicrous though it seems in this heat. He's going to stay behind and cross his fingers there's no emergency work, and I'll do the clinic flight.'

Janet didn't know whether to feel glad or sorry. She reflected ruefully that she didn't feel fully at ease with either of Benanda's doctors. That was unusual for her, as, although fairly quiet, she usually got on well with most people. She could not help blaming herself for it, too. She should never have responded so strongly to Paul in Sydney, and as for her reaction to Clifford's kiss . . . She was having to try very hard to squash the turmoil within her whenever she saw him. Somehow the heat didn't help, either.

This time John Hunt took the seat next to Bill, and the dental nurse and Janet and Clifford squeezed into the back. Conditions were a little cramped and Jill said that she would occupy the stretcher and catch up on some missed sleep. That left Clifford and Janet to sit together on the narrow seats. She sat in the one next to the window and took refuge from the need for conversation by staring out of it. In any case, the plane was very noisy.

Janet had become used to flying in the Piper Chieftain by now, having made several flights in it for minor emergencies, as well as her first clinic flight and the trip to assist Mrs Pooley with her birth at Coolingee. She had never been afraid of flying, and quite enjoyed the exhilaration of landing and take-off, even on the bumpiest of outback airstrips.

While the plane was in the air, it was easiest to think, take in the view lazily, or doze. In this weather, the plane was one of the coolest places there was, and having had a few hot and restless nights lately, Janet felt herself grow drowsy under the influence of the engine's steady drone . . .

She jerked awake just as her head came into contact with Clifford's shoulder, and straightened herself again, embarrassed. Fortunately, the plane was coming in to land now, at the first of their stops. But he had not missed the moment.

'Your light-headedness must have passed,' he said. 'For the first few days after your hair-cut, I wondered if you even managed to anchor your head to the pillow at night.'

'Did it show?' Janet asked, surprised that he had noticed her appearance at all during that time. He had given no sign of it. 'I know it felt very light, but . . .'

'It did show,' he nodded. 'It still does, in a way. You move your head much more, and that hair swings round like a bell. It was beautiful before, so thick and heavy and glossy, but I think after all I like it better now. How do you feel about it?'

'Oh . . . I'm used to it. I like it, too. It's amazing, really. I thought it would take a lot longer.' Janet's reply was awkward. She hated talking to him about her hair. It reminded her that all of their most emotional moments together—both angry and intimate—seemed to have been sparked off by it.

Now, for instance, he was still looking at her thoughtfully.

'It gives you a boyish, Twenties look that suits your personality.'

'Do you know me well enough to say that?' Janet returned, putting a little distance in her tone.

'Perhaps not. I wasn't suggesting I did. It was just an impression,' was his answer, distant too.

The Piper Chieftain bumped to the ground just then, and they both became fully occupied in their work, seeing several patients each and finishing after John and Jill had completed their dental work. The property, Bannon Park, was a small one, but two carloads of people had driven across from a bush pub fifteen miles away, and three of them needed both dental and medical treatment.

Their next stop, where lunch was served, was busy too, and it was only when they took off after it that Janet realised she had not even asked where they would be spending the night.

'It's a place called Moollawindra,' Clifford said, passing the map across to her and pointing.

'Moollawindra!' Janet exclaimed. 'But I thought that was in Charleville Base's area.'

'It used to be. We've only taken it over from Charleville in the past year,' Clifford answered, then stopped. 'But why? Do you know it?'

Janet was on the point of nodding and explaining, but suddenly a vision of it rose in her mind's eye. Moollawindra! Ten years since she had seen it, now. So many special memories connected with the place. Would it have changed? Soon she would see it and know, and tonight she would be able to explore it thoroughly, and with adult eyes.

Suddenly she didn't want to tell Clifford about her

past. It seemed that either Paul had not mentioned it, or
Clifford had forgotten that it was Moollawindra where
she had spent her childhood.

'I've . . . I mean, some relations of mine used to own
it,' she said. It wasn't quite a lie, and sometime she might
tell him the full story, but today she wanted to see her
old home without another's eye observing her every
reaction. Emotional moments were not things she
liked to share with everybody.

They landed at a little before five, after another long
stop at a place called Wingamurtee, where Janet recognised an aboriginal stockman, now too old to work, who
had been employed for years at Moollawindra. The
country at Wingamurtee had seemed familiar, too. They
were in Southern Queensland and the soil wasn't so red.

Moollawindra was instantly familiar, even from the
air, as they came in to land. The heat was still intense
when they stepped from the plane at the end of the
barren airstrip. Janet remembered that it had been built
at quite a distance from the house—nearly a mile—on a
slight ridge.

She thought of Stephanie Beddie's shuddering comment about Diri Diri being 'a hundred miles from nowhere'. The description fitted Moollawindra very well.
Janet realised that she had never talked much with her
mother about life out here. How had it been for the
young woman from the town of Cunnamulla when she
had first come out here as a new wife twenty-five years
ago?

Janet wondered about Stephanie Beddie's mysterious
stay down south and her sudden return. What was
Clifford's connection with all that? And had Janet's own
mother ever wanted to run away?

A freckled, gangling young stockman waited by his
land-rover to drive them to the homestead. Janet
studied his face covertly but could not recognise him. He
only looked about twenty, which meant he would just
have been an urchin of ten when she had lived here, and

it seemed likely that he had come here from some small town like Windorah or Birdsville.

But she realised that she would have to steel herself to recognise one or two people at least over the next few hours—some of the aboriginals, perhaps, who lived on the property. She might even be recognised herself, although probably she had changed too much, and her hair had been long at thirteen, too.

There was little conversation in the baking interior of the landrover. Everyone was much too tired and drained after the overpowering heat of the day, and was looking forward to the time an hour or so hence when they could down tools and cool off with a shower before an iced drink and a meal.

Janet had to suppress an interest in her surroundings which would have struck the others as unusual, but even so, she caught Clifford's eye more than once and wondered if there was something significant in the way he was watching her.

The homestead and scattered out-buildings did seem different. They were less spread out than her memory had told her, and she supposed it was a child's view that was fixed in her mind, when distances seemed greater and buildings taller.

The garden had changed too. The new owners—the Fosters—had given up her mother's painstakingly cultivated kitchen garden and replaced it with a small lawn and barbecue area, shaded by shrubs and a white-trunked ghost gum, all of which seemed to be doing well enough on water pumped from the artesian bore a hundred yards away.

John Hunt, assisted by Jill, did his dental work inside the house, but Clifford and Janet were shown to a room in an outbuilding, which Janet remembered as having been the dry goods store, but which was now used as a craft-room by Mrs Foster.

Janet saw Max Foster first. He was a weather-beaten man in his early fifties, and Clifford had told her that he was at risk of having a heart attack in the next few years, so the check-up she gave him was thorough—blood-pressure, pulse and questions about diet, stress and smoking. There were some rough spots on his hands and face, too, which Janet suspected were keratoses—spots of skin cancer. She asked Clifford to look at them after he had finished examining Mrs Foster and he confirmed her idea.

'I've been watching them for a few months,' he said, after Mr and Mrs Foster had left the make-shift surgery. 'He and his wife are going to Sydney in February for a holiday. He's booked into a skin specialist there, who'll remove them with a new liquid nitrogen technique they've been using recently. Skin cancer is a common enough problem with fair-skinned people in this region, unfortunately.'

'It's not a very serious type, though, is it?' Janet asked.

'No, it's not melanoma. You can be quite sure that I keep a good lookout for that. In a city, a specialist would make the diagnosis, but out here . . . I've done quite a lot of reading about it. There was one case last year—a simple mole on a man's knee, quite a young man, too—but if we hadn't got to it in time, that patient would have died within months.'

'Surely with the research that's being done into more effective blockout creams . . .' Janet began.

'You just try getting some of these die-hard bushmen to put cream on their hands and faces,' Clifford laughed ruefully. 'But of course awareness of melanoma is increasing, and I think the younger generation is taking more care.'

They saw several more patients after this but the conversation stayed in Janet's mind. It seemed to have become the way they got on best of late, having talks of this sort—safe talks about subjects closely related to work. In fact, they were a good team as doctor and nurse, both fairly quiet people who liked to work in an atmosphere of calm concentration, putting personal affairs completely to one side, apart from a bit of light gossip with talkative patients.

They finished work at half past six, and found that John and Jill were just emerging after their session too, having made one extraction and done several fillings, as well as giving check-ups to healthy mouths.

'Whew! I think I'm going to be too tired to eat,' John Hunt said. 'What time's dinner, do you know? Is there time for a lie-down beforehand?'

'They usually eat at about eight here in the hot weather,' Clifford said. 'It's dark and cooler by then.'

'I don't feel like a lie-down,' Jill said. 'But some kind of relaxing thing would be nice.'

They all stood on the wide screened-in verandah at the front of the homestead. Max Foster had returned to one of the farther outbuildings to complete some work, and his wife was in the kitchen making preparations for the barbecue they were to eat that evening. She had already insisted that she did not need any help and had told the professional visitors to unwind in any way they chose until cool drinks were served at a quarter to eight.

This verandah had scarcely changed. Its varnished floorboards were the same colour, and it provided the same cool contrast with the backing yard outside where a few cattle dogs flicked their tails lazily, stretched out in a shaded corner. The scene reminded Janet inevitably of the many summer evenings she had spent here, filling in time between a late swim and the evening meal.

'What about a swim in the waterhole?' she said suddenly.

'Is there one?' Jill asked. She was fairly new to the job and had not been here before.

'Yes there is,' Janet said unthinkingly. 'Down past the . . . I mean, I noticed the trees marking the course of the river. I thought this summer after the rain it would be flowing.'

'There is a waterhole,' Clifford nodded. 'And a swim

sounds like a fine idea to me. In fact, I imagine that's where Bill is already. But did anyone bring their costumes?'

'Oh! No, I didn't,' Janet said.

'Me neither,' Jill nodded, then added, 'We could be modern I suppose, and go without.'

'Not for me,' John Hunt said hastily. 'I'll stick to my siesta plan.'

'I'd really love a swim,' Janet said hesitantly. 'But what about towels?'

'Cynthia will lend us those,' Clifford said, and went immediately to ask her, returning a few minutes later with three brightly-coloured old beach towels.

'See you later then,' John Hunt said, heading off along the verandah to the covered walkway which led to the stockmen's quarters where they were all to spend the night.

The other three left the shade of the verandah and crossed the yard. Clifford led the way, taking a route that was very familiar to Janet, but beyond the wooden-railed stockyards, she saw that he looked uncertain about where to go. A wide sweep of trees about fifty yards away marked the curved course of the river, but in this dry region, even in a summer that followed plentiful rains, the current was no longer flowing and there was just one pool at Moollawindra that was deep and fresh enough to swim in.

Two tracks led away from the homestead in the direction of the belt of trees. One went to the bore outlet and dam, and the other to a shed where old farm machinery was stored, but one of the two also led beyond, to the swimming spot. Which? Clifford clearly didn't know. Janet did. For a moment she hesitated, then plunged in.

'This one.' She began to walk along the machinery shed track. Clifford wasn't following.

'It looks further from the river,' he said. 'I think it's the other track.'

'It isn't,' Janet said, making the decision to be honest. 'I know. I remember . . . from my childhood, when I lived here.'

'You lived here? You dark horse! You didn't say anything about it before,' Jill exclaimed frankly.

Janet risked a glance at Clifford. He was looking at her, clearly very surprised and uncomprehending. She regretted her reticence now. It had only made things more awkward. He would wonder why she had said nothing until now and it would be too hard to explain her odd need for a private exploration of her memories. What would he say?

They walked in silence for a few minutes down the rough double-rutted track, their feet thudding dully on the pinkish-brown baked clay surface. Janet walked quickly, both to get out of the sun sooner and to keep ahead of Clifford and avoid his gaze. But she realised that her behaviour would only arouse more curiosity in her two companions, so she slowed down and prepared herself to speak.

'I didn't want to say anything about it before. It's hard to explain. I wanted to see how much it had changed. I didn't want people asking questions about my memories and my feelings. That's silly I suppose.'

Unconsciously, she had been speaking mostly to Clifford, and Jill had stopped to examine an interesting stone lying by the side of the track, as if she had assumed that it was a private conversation between the two of them.

'It's not silly,' Clifford said, and Janet remembered that he had used those words to her before, after she had cried about her hair. 'It's obviously a memory that's very important to you. Of course you couldn't tell everyone about it as though you were making small talk. I could see that you were taken by surprise to find we were coming here today, and . . . well . . . I've come to realise that you're not someone who likes to talk much about your feelings.'

'No . . .'

'How long did you live here?'

'The first thirteen years of my life,' Janet replied. 'I told Paul. That was the reason I wanted the job at Benanda—to return to the desert and see it with adult eyes. I thought Paul would have told you.'

'No, he didn't,' Clifford said. What Paul *had* said was that in Sydney at a party he had met 'a little charmer of a nurse', who was looking for a bit of a change, but Janet's words had altered Clifford's perception of his nurse once and for all.

'Here we are then,' Janet said brightly. When Clifford was gentle and understanding like this, it became too hard to remember that she didn't trust him, and that she disapproved of his relationships with Stephanie Beddie and Marcia Fairfax.

Jill had caught up to them again and was showing them her stone, which was dark red, dense and smooth, with angular chips flaked from it.

'Keep it,' Clifford said. 'And show it to the Fosters. I'm not in any way an expert, but it looks as though it's an aboriginal tool. Max Foster has a collection of them and knows quite a lot about it. There's a lot of skill in those implements, though this one seems to have been rejected before it was finished.'

Janet scrambled down the steep bank ahead of the others, relieved that the talk had taken a lighter tone again. Instinctively, she headed for the flat spot where some grass grew and where they had always laid out their towels as children. The Fosters had built a little wooden jetty at this point, which jutted out into the water and provided a place to dive from and sunbake on, as well as a launching point for boats.

Bill Kirkely was standing on it, still wet and shirtless.

'Just got me daks on in time,' he said, with a wicked grin. 'I didn't realise you lot were coming down.'

'We haven't got bathers either,' Janet confessed, a little embarrassed.

'Don't worry,' Bill said, picking up his towel. 'I'm heading back now to do a few checks on the plane. The water's great though. You'll enjoy it.'

He left, and the other three laid down their towels. The waterhole was at its fullest, as the river was only just beginning to dry up. It was a deep, tranquil pool, well shaded by trees, and about a hundred yards long by thirty wide. It very seldom dried up completely, and though it was the colour of weak milky tea, that was universal in this area and everyone soon forgot that rivers could be any other colour.

'Mmm! I can't wait,' Jill said, gazing appreciatively at the water, then she voiced Janet's private thought. 'It's a bit embarrassing, isn't it? I've never swum in my birthday suit in mixed company before. Still, in the age of Aquarius . . .'

She kicked off sandals, peeled off her blue uniform, slipped out of scanty underclothes and splashed into the water. Janet started to do the same, trying not to be aware, out of the corner of her eye, of the brown and white blur that was Clifford's body about to enter the water. He made his usual expert, almost soundless dive and began to swim with confident strokes towards the centre of the pool.

A moment later, Janet was in the water as well, gasping with delight at the instant refreshment it gave to her overheated body. It was actually delicious to swim naked and feel the water relaxing every muscle and every tired pore in her skin. She forgot the slight self-consciousness she had felt as they undressed as she swam like a porpoise, diving deep and resurfacing, rolling on to her back and kicking, splashing with child-like exuberance in shallower water.

Jill swam to the other side, rested there for a moment, then kicked lazily across again on her back. After this exercise, she seemed content to bob quietly beneath the shade of an overhanging tree. Clifford swam back and forth several times then came towards Janet and they trod water together at one of the deepest parts in the middle.

'Pity there's no tree to dive from like at Benanda.'

'Yes,' Janet nodded. 'There used to be a rope from that tree on the far bank. We swung from it all the time, but it's gone now, and the branch it hung from is too high to dive off.'

'Let's do the length and back. Is that possible?' Clifford asked.

'Yes, we used to do it. There weren't any snags then. It's about a hundred yards.'

'Four Olympic pool lengths then. That'll have our hearts pumping,' Clifford said.

They set off from their point in the middle, both using a capable freestyle stroke. They stopped and rested on the stony bed at the second end, panting but exhilarated.

'Jill seems to have gone,' Clifford observed.

'Yes . . .' Janet nodded. So now she was alone with Clifford!

'She probably called but we didn't hear her,' he said. 'Perhaps we should head back too. We've been here a while.'

Janet nodded, still breathless. The water was clearer in this shallow part, and she was aware of the pale distorted outline of their bodies. Now that Jill had gone, she felt less comfortable with him. The shadows had been long before. Now the sun was almost completely gone and the water was in shade. Evening sounds were beginning in the trees around them, but they were not human sounds. There were only their two selves here in the water, close enough to touch . . .

'I'll race you to the jetty,' she said, and struck off at once to give herself a head start. He beat her, but not by much, and they clung to the wooden supports of the jetty panting and laughing for a few moments, before he hauled his long body up out of the water . . .

Janet swam away from the jetty to the sloping bank and got out there, by which time Clifford was already towelling himself vigorously. He glanced at her quickly as she stood up out of the water, streaming wet, but then turned away, leaving Janet hot with awareness. She reached quickly for her own towel and was soon safely wrapped in it.

'Look at you rubbing at that mop-top,' he teased a minute or two later when he was dressed again in his khaki pants, though his tanned torso was still bare and damp. 'You might have had that wash-and-wear look all your life.'

'It's lovely,' she admitted, flushing slightly. She was using both ends of the towel to rub her hair, which left it open in the middle and she was only facing half away from him. She turned a little more.

'I do feel much freer,' she continued. 'I hadn't realised quite how much time and effort I had to spend on it. It had been long since I was eleven.'

She retrieved underclothes, sandals and the striped sundress she had brought to change into and put them on, not looking at him, then gathered her towel and soiled uniform and they were ready to leave. A silence had fallen between them now, and was interrupted only once during the walk back.

'That was lovely,' Clifford said.

'Perfect,' Janet agreed.

CHAPTER SEVEN

A DUST storm howled violently around Moollawindra homestead, a sinister dust storm that seemed almost like a living being in its malignancy. Janet shuddered at the sound of the shrieking winds. She didn't want to hear them, and yet for some reason she had to listen very hard. But no, it wasn't the wind she had to listen to, it was more something she was listening for above the wind.

Suddenly her mother was there.

'But you're at the beach with Tony and Catherine,' Janet heard herself say, bewildered.

'I came back with your father.' Her mother's voice sounded strange. It sounded like Janet's teacher on the School of the Air, who was also for some reason the Matron at South Sydney Hospital.

'I didn't know you were a nurse, Mum,' Janet said.

'It's because of your father,' her mother explained, still in Sister McCredie's voice, but urgently now. 'You must go and find the plane at once, or he'll die. I know he'll die.'

Janet looked at her father on the couch and saw that her mother was right. She had to find the plane. But she couldn't see anything in the storm. The dust and darkness had come inside now and she had to push against them with all her might even to get to the door. And yet she had to get there. She had to. She could hear the plane. It was out there somewhere. She was pushing towards it. Clifford was flying it and she had to let him know that her father was lying here ill, before the plane took off without him. If she could just call out loudly enough above the storm so that Clifford would wake. If she could just call 'Clifford! Clifford!' so that he heard his name, the plane would stay . . .

A real sound, the sound of the door opening and closing, cut across the nightmare shrieking of the wind in Janet's dream. For a moment, the sound became part of the dream—she had got the door open at last to go outside to the plane—then she felt strong arms around her and Clifford was there, his voice quiet and reassuring.

'Wake up, Janet. Sit up and forget the dream. I'm here.'

'Was it a dream? Oh, of course it was. For a while it was so real!'

The desert night had cooled quickly, and she shivered momentarily in her thin mauve cotton nightdress.

'You were calling my name,' Clifford said. He was sitting on the bed and Janet could feel the warmth of his thighs and hips against her legs through the white sheet. His bare arms were around her too, and he wore only silk pyjama pants in pale avocado green.

'Yes,' she nodded, trying not to be aware of all this. 'You were flying the plane and I was scared you wouldn't wait. My father had had his heart attack, and there was a dust storm, and my mother wanted me to find the plane—only she wasn't really my mother, she was Sister McCredie from South Sydney, and . . . oh, it was all very stupid.'

'But understandable,' Clifford said, his face close to hers, its features only faintly visible in the dimness. 'Coming here for the first time in ten years, telling us about some of your memories, and about your father's heart trouble over dinner. And you drank some red wine. Listen! There is even some wind now to suggest the dust storm to you in your sleep. It's not surprising that you should have had a nightmare.'

'I feel like a kid of ten,' Janet laughed, embarrassed, now that she was fully awake, by the fact that he had had to come and comfort her like this. Without her wanting it, images of their swim together kept filling her mind . . .

'It's not like a kid that I'm feeling right at this moment,' Clifford said meaningfully, echoing Janet's own awareness.

He twisted his legs up and on to the bed and stretched them out, then tightened his hold on her and nuzzled the curve of her neck. Janet felt a warm tingle ripple through her at the touch of his lips and the feel of his warm breath. He slid her down on to the pillow and found her lips, travelling across from her neck and leaving a burning trail in the wake of his kisses. Janet's arms came around his shoulders and she threaded her fingers through his clean thick hair.

They rolled together, lost in feverish exploration without thought of what it might mean. Their long swim before sunset had given a freshness and firmness to Janet's skin, and she felt her every nerve-ending alive with a delightful warm sensation as he caressed her.

But why was he doing this? It was in imminent danger of going too far here in this dark room with no one to interrupt them, and he had spoken no words about his feelings for her.

What was this attraction that could flare so quickly between them? Something merely physical? Something that came from loneliness? A product of the desert with its savage ability to intensify all emotions?

'Clifford, no!' Janet pulled away. 'Please . . . no.'

Clifford groaned and turned his head aside, burying it in the pillow, and above the sound he made, Janet heard another noise that sounded like hurried footsteps. But she had to be mistaken. It was the middle of the night. Then an insistent knocking came to her ears.

'Clifford! Dr Ransome!' It was Max Foster and he was hammering urgently at the door of the doctor's room, which was next to Janet's own. She looked at him, but he did not move, simply made another sound and burrowed deeper into her pillow. He wasn't asleep though. Far from it.

Janet's nightdress was caught beneath him. She pulled it free and went to her door as Max Foster knocked and called again.

'Clifford's in here, Mr Foster,' she said with a composure she did not feel in the least. He turned away from Clifford's door, startled at the sound of her unexpected voice. Then the doctor was behind Janet.

'What's the problem, Max?'

'Sorry, I didn't . . .' The older man looked from one to the other, clearly embarrassed.

'It doesn't matter.' Clifford's voice was cool, controlled and steady. 'Just tell me what's wrong.'

'Martin Baird just made contact with the emergency signal through the transceiver from Benanda. There's been a shooting accident just beyond the eastern boundary of Moollawindra. Martin thought it would be quicker to contact you. It's a couple of roo shooters, and apparently they're on the edge of a claypan. It's baked like rock in this weather, so you could land quite easily . . .'

'Wake Bill, would you?' Clifford was wasting no time now. 'I'll be dressed in a minute and you too please, Janet.'

Not a hint remained of his earlier caressing tone, and Janet was very glad of it. She knew exactly what Max Foster must be thinking, and he wasn't too far wrong. She felt hideous about it now, and just wanted to get back to some kind of rational state as soon as possible. In a way, the emergency that faced them, although it sounded both serious and messy, would provide a much-needed opportunity for her to recover her even keel.

She disappeared into her own room as Clifford had done, put on a clean if slightly crumpled uniform, and brushed her short hair quickly. When she emerged, Bill was up and dressed, and Clifford was ready too.

'What do I need to do now?' Max Foster was saying.

'Give us some light on the airstrip,' Bill said. 'Two vehicles if possible, with their headlights shining down the strip. Is Cynthia awake?'

'Yes. She's waiting to see what's happening. She'll drive the other vehicle.'

He went off at a lope, with a country man's athleticism in spite of his years and the beginning of the heart trouble which reminded Janet so strongly of her father. Bill, Clifford and Janet went to wait in the landrover and they set off as soon as he arrived with the keys, at a pace which jolted every bone in Janet's body. The three of them climbed into the plane while Max Foster swung the wheel of the rattling vehicle to drive it to the end of the strip so that its lights shone straight along. Mrs Foster arrived just as Bill was taxiing into position, and with the light from the two vehicles, the airstrip was illuminated reasonably well.

Janet was relieved to find herself alone in her usual back-seat position. She just didn't want to be close to Clifford, with the awareness that would bring of their interrupted passion. The atmosphere in the front seat was tense and there was little unnecessary conversation. Was it just that Clifford was thinking of the emergency work that lay ahead?

A thin veil of cloud had formed in the sky, but behind it, a half moon shone, helping Bill to see his way. The instrument panels were lit up, and the engine roared then settled into a steady hum. Max Foster had been able to pinpoint the roo shooters' whereabouts on a map, after listening to their description, relayed by Martin, of the claypan they were on and the track they had taken, and he had given the co-ordinates to Bill.

It was only a short flight and before they had had time to gain any height, they were descending towards the inky blackness of the earth again. At the last moment, Janet could make out the faint pale glow of the hard-surfaced claypan and then they were down on it, braking hard and bumping over the clumps of emu bush that grew at intervals. When they had reached a controlled speed, Bill taxied around, telling Clifford and Janet to keep a close watch for the lights of the roo shooters' truck, which would be switched on to indicate their position in the deserted landscape.

'There! Just beyond the edge of the claypan to the right,' Janet exclaimed a minute later.

'At four o'clock, she means,' Clifford put in.

Bill taxied the plane towards the light that filtered through some low stunted trees beyond the claypan, and then they saw a figure emerge and wave frantically. Soon the doctor and Janet were on the ground, running to meet the man. Bill stayed in the plane, trying to plot the best direction for take-off. Into the wind was best, but was the claypan long enough in that direction? They had landed almost at right angles to it . . .

'He's in the truck,' the roo shooter said. 'I couldn't get it any closer.'

'Where is the wound?' Clifford questioned him urgently.

'In his thigh. I did it. It was an accident. We were reloading and . . .'

'Save your explanations.' Clifford cut across his words. 'Has he lost much blood?'

'Looks like a lot. I don't know. He's my brother. He's got to be all right.'

They had been heading towards the truck parked in the scrub as they talked. Janet carried a bag of equipment and Clifford had the fold-up stretcher, which could certainly be needed. With a thigh wound, the injured man would find walking almost impossible.

They heard his groans well before they reached the truck. When they did reach it, Janet could not help shuddering at the bloody kangaroo carcasses strung in the back. She knew that a certain number had to be culled, but that did not make it any easier to witness, and she supported groups who were lobbying to get greater controls put on the industry to ensure that the killing was done humanely, and that rare species were strictly protected.

She must have come across roo shooters in her childhood, but had no recollections of it. Certainly, this was the first time she had seen the way they lived and worked at first hand. It must be a lonely, violent and difficult life, combing the bush like this at the dead of night.

'They're here, Ted,' his brother called, but there was no reply—or at least, not in words. The injured man continued to groan and Janet thought that she caught the word 'water' somewhere in his sounds.

'Do you have water?' she asked the man who moved just ahead of her. He turned, his eyes distracted looking and his face unshaven after two nights in the bush.

'There's a jerry-can in the back of the truck,' he said.

'Matt . . .' The injured man called. 'The blood's through that rag now.'

Clifford was at the passenger door of the truck, taking a sterile packet of gauze bandage from the bag of equipment they had brought. He bent over the wound then straightened abruptly with a muttered word.

'You haven't cut away his trouser leg?' It was part question, part exclamation.

'No,' Matt replied. 'It was bleeding so hard. I just tied that rag on top.'

'We can't waste any more time now then,' Clifford said shortly. 'We'll have to clean it up in the plane.'

Janet had found the water and soaked a piece of bandage in it for Ted to suck, while Clifford was working.

'I don't think it's hit bone,' he said. 'You're very lucky.'

When the bandage was secured with tape, he prepared the stretcher, and then, with Janet's help, eased the injured shooter onto it.

'Matt—you'll help me carry him. Janet, bring the bag would you?'

The return trip to the plane was slower of course, as

the terrain was rough under foot, and the injured
man was a burly fellow, but they made it as quickly as
possible and he was soon loaded into the rear of the
plane.

'Broken Hill, Bill,' Clifford said. 'He's going to need a
transfusion, and there's a risk of infection too.'

'Will he be all right?' was Matt's last hoarse question
to Janet before the door of the Piper Chieftain was
closed.

'Looks like it.' She didn't want to be one hundred
percent confident. The man had lost a lot of blood, and,
she suspected suddenly from the smell on his breath,
both he and his brother had been drinking.

Janet and Clifford were now crouched at his side in the
back of the plane. It would have been an uncomfortable
position if they had not been so pre-occupied. Taxiing
and take-off were both rough and Bill swore tensely and
absent-mindedly several times as he wrestled with the
controls.

Ted was silent—eyes closed, forehead damp with
sweat.

'I think he's lost consciousness,' Clifford said. 'In a
way it's for the best. What I'm going to do is going to
hurt. Pass Box 2A please, Janet.'

She did so, then busied herself with trying to antici-
pate the doctor's every move so that she was ready with
whatever information or equipment he needed. Clifford
worked in silence now. After injecting a pain-killing
drug, he cut away the filthy trouser-leg, unwrapped the
gauze bandage and cleaned the wound with antiseptic.
He staunched as much of the blood flow as he could by
using closure clips, and wound a new bandage tightly
across the wound. Janet was ready with kidney bowl and
swabs, and managed to take the patient's pulse as well. It
was very poor, but soon she noticed signs of increasing
life.

'I think he's coming round.'

'There's a lot of foreign matter in the wound,' Clifford

said. 'I'd almost like to start getting it out now, but with the blood he's already lost . . .'

Janet waited, thinking of what equipment she would have to have ready if he did decide to risk opening the wound further.

'No,' he decided finally. 'Of the two risks, infection's the least.'

'I think he'd been drinking. Did you . . . ?' Janet began.

'Yes, I'm bearing that in mind, don't worry. Benanda Base has run into this pair before. They rolled their truck a year or so back. Matt got a bad break in his arm. And I don't suppose this will be the last accident they're involved in. They're not typical of all roo shooters, thank goodness, and they've kept their damage to themselves so far.'

'Still . . . It's a hard life,' Janet said, groping for an understanding of the lives some men chose.

'Yes,' Clifford nodded, then looked sharply at her. 'You do understand the outback, don't you?'

'Perhaps,' Janet answered. 'Although . . . does anyone?'

'Maybe not.'

After this, there was a long silence between them against the backdrop of the engine's noise. Each was quietly aware of every change in the condition of the patient, but there was time for other awareness now, too. Janet caught a glimpse of Clifford's watch. Nearly four. She had lost all feeling of the passage of time, but guessed that it must be about an hour—or more?—since Max Foster had called them.

Her face burned again as she thought of what Max Foster would have assumed, and there was a sudden stabbing warmth deep in her torso as she remembered the fire that Clifford's caresses and the pressure of his long body had kindled inside her. Did he have any idea that she had responded so strongly.

Janet risked a glance at him and was disconcerted to

find his compassionate yet fiery brown eyes already upon her. She flushed and looked down again, pretending to find a piece of equipment that needed re-arranging. He wanted to speak. She could see it and was suddenly afraid of what he might say and of what her own response might be.

If he said 'Let's forget it' as he had said once before, she didn't want to hear. They could each reach the decision to 'forget it' without the words needing to be spoken. If he wanted to propose . . . what? some kind of affair—then she just wasn't interested. She had a good store of pride, while he had two women at his beck and call already. She didn't want an apology either.

So what did she want? At that moment the patient stirred, groaned and opened his eyes. Clifford bent over him to murmur some reassuring words in his deep vibrant-toned voice. And it was then that Janet knew the answer to her question.

She wanted him to say that he loved her, that he had finished with Stephanie Beddie and Marcia Fairfax, that somehow Janet had misunderstood the whole situation and it was herself he cared for in a way that was not simply physical . . .

'Janet, are you all right?' Clifford's voice came, low and professionally concerned.

'Just tired I suppose.' She found a smile, but did not meet his eyes.

'Yes, it's been . . . a long night.' He sighed through a tight throat, and for a moment Janet thought that he might have been referring to their time together in her room. 'A shooting accident isn't pretty, either. But we'll be in Broken Hill soon.'

Janet nodded as politeness demanded, fighting the sudden growth of misery inside her. It was appalling to find that she felt so strongly about Clifford. Tonight's passion between them had made a difference, had cemented something in her heart, and of course he wasn't going to say any of those last things she had imagined.

It was Stephanie he cared about, Stephanie whose marriage he might soon break up. Janet, like Marcia Fairfax, was an interim measure, it seemed, to quiet his physical needs. She felt used and knew she should hate him, but somehow she couldn't. She remembered what Jill had said before their swim that afternoon about 'being modern'.

Perhaps the situation between Clifford, Stephanie and Marcia was 'modern' too, and completely understood and accepted by each of them. Perhaps Marcia wanted a very light physical relationship as Clifford did. And perhaps Clifford thought that Janet felt the same. It was the way some people did conduct their lives these days, she knew—one-night stands, brief casual 'flings'. But it was not for Janet. It affronted something in her nature and she knew that she could never separate love from physical commitment.

'Why don't you sit back and try to relax for a while?' Clifford's voice cut across these bitter, uncertain thoughts. 'I'll keep an eye on Ted. It doesn't need two of us. You'll find it tough getting through the rest of the clinic flight if you don't rest.'

'But what about you . . . ?'

'I'll manage.'

Janet took up his suggestion, more because it would be easier to be at a distance from him than because she thought she would relax or sleep in the short time that remained before they landed.

Yet surprisingly, she did slip into a doze, lulled by the thrum of the engine. Bill had radioed in to Broken Hill hospital to tell them about the accident, and an ambulance was already waiting on the tarmac as they touched down at the near-deserted airport.

After this, events moved very fast. The injured man was loaded straight from the plane into the ambulance, and Janet began to clamber out of the plane herself. But

Clifford stopped her at the door.

'I'll go with him. No need for you to come.'

'But . . .'

'You're *not needed*,' he stressed. 'Stay here and get some rest while you can.'

He put out a lean hand and touched her hair in a quick caress that was instantly disturbing. Janet shivered away from his touch and saw him frown and stiffen. He had interpreted her movement as a rejection. So much the better.

He had gone almost before she could complete the thought. The ambulance moved off, its red lights cutting swathes across the tarmac, and then a minute later in the distance Janet heard the wail of its sirens start up as it came onto the public road.

It was quiet on the tarmac now. Bill had sloped off to the terminal building for coffee and a yarn with someone else who was working the graveyard shift. The spare stretcher beckoned invitingly and Janet was soon stretched out on it. She wouldn't sleep. She wanted to think over what she was going to do about this new unmistakable feeling for Clifford, and be awake ready to hear news of the injured man when Clifford returned from the hospital . . .

Later, she was dimly aware of the light of dawn filtering into the plane, of the sound of the Piper Chieftain's engine starting up, and of the movement of take-off, but it was not until Clifford leaned over and spoke her name that she woke properly. He was smiling at her with mild amusement.

'Surfaced?'

'Almost.' She could not help smiling back, although there was a new stab of pain, now, every time she met his gaze.

'You obviously needed it.'

'How is Ted?' That was a safe subject, and one which concerned her.

'He's going to be fine. I waited a little longer than

necessary to make sure. There was no problem in matching his blood type, and his blood alcohol level had subsided below danger point. They're operating to extract the bullet . . . Indeed,' he glanced at his watch, 'they might well be finished.'

'Breakfast at Moollawindra,' Bill said with relish as he began the plane's descent.

'Mmm, a good big bush breakfast, too,' Clifford put in.

Janet said nothing. Back to Moollawindra! It could only be a few hours since they had left, and only a little over twelve hours since she had swum naked with Clifford in the old waterhole of her childhood. Janet felt that she had done a lot of living in those twelve hours.

'I can't go on feeling like this about Clifford,' she said to herself as they came in to land and she found herself staring helplessly at the back of his dark head. 'Not when it's so hopeless, and when I have to see him all the time as though everything's quite normal. I've just got to forget about it. It will get easier . . .'

CHAPTER EIGHT

DID it become easier? Perhaps. Janet could not suspend her life because she found herself so painfully in love with Clifford, and the weeks had their ups and downs much the same as ever. The sun's heat was now at its highest, and it laid an extra quality of feeling over everything. Lorna had rummaged out an electric fan for Janet and she usually kept it on at night, and when she was at home during the day. It stirred the air a little, and gave at least the illusion of coolness.

In her time off there were outings: swimming at the river, occasionally with Paul, often with Iris Connolly —never with Clifford Ransome; lunch out at Fairwater Park, on a day when Marcia was not at home; the promised trip out to Pat Jackson's property, Walkaninna Creek. Janet knew that Pat was interested in her, and worried that she might be encouraging him unfairly by agreeing that it would be nice to go out there again when the cooler weather arrived and they could go riding. If she could make it clear to Pat that it was only friendship she wanted, he would make a good friend. But while her feeling for Clifford burned inside her like this, it couldn't be anything more than friendship.

Lorna was still making her batches of summer produce, and Janet filled other spare hours with knitting two pretty pastel-toned cotton tops, playing music on her small cassette player, or simply sitting in the shade of Lorna's verandah with a book and a long iced drink.

But it was work which absorbed her far more than leisure time. The emergency flights she made with Clifford and Paul—and she seemed to spend about equal time with each of the two doctors these days— covered the whole of Benanda Base's sector. Many were minor, and treatment could be given on the spot, but others took all her concentration and effort, and involved tense evacuation flights to Benanda, Broken Hill and occasionally as far as Adelaide.

Janet much preferred to fly with Paul these days, although they didn't work so well together. She liked to remain as cool as possible in a crisis, while he was, by unpredictable turns, lively and jocular or bad-tempered and abrupt. Clifford's quiet, business-like ways suited Janet better—or would have done if she could ever feel at ease in his presence.

It was terribly hard to watch his quick careful hands at work and not remember the magic they had worked on her own body that dramatic night at Moollawindra, hard not to scan his face in search of some kind of warmth and deeper feeling which her reason told her bluntly she would not find there.

But she won these battles, and found after a while that she was refusing to look at him even when politeness required it. He would think her strangely prickly and cold, but that was better than having him guess the truth—that she was fighting a love for him that grew deeper every day, and that she would have gone to him openly, in some moods, if he had asked it of her, in spite of all she knew about Stephanie Beddie and Marcia Fairfax . . .

It was one morning in mid-February when she heard Stephanie's voice over the transceiver as she was bringing in a glass of iced orange juice for Clifford, who sat at the controls giving his batch of morning radio consultations.

It was unusual to hear Diri Diri over the airwaves. Mostly they didn't seem to take part in the 'Galah' session, and Janet thought that if Stephanie Beddie was lonely 'a hundred miles from nowhere', it was at least partly her own fault for not becoming involved in the community life of the region in this way. Was it that she was not popular with the other men and women who took part in the long-distance conversations? Or was she trying to keep aloof from them?

'Clifford? Is that you?' came the familiar slightly helpless tones, only slightly distorted by the airwaves, in answer to Clifford's identification code-word.

'Yes, Stephanie.'

At once his tone was guarded and he cast a swift glance over his shoulder at Janet, who was just about to put down his dewed glass. She almost dropped it, spilling a drip or two on some papers in front of him and murmuring a garbled apology for her clumsiness in response to his quick frown, before beating a too-hasty retreat.

He must not think that she was in any way curious to hear the conversation—although of course she was, in spite of her many resolves to steer clear of the whole thing. Whatever was going on between Clifford and Stephanie, it was quite clearly *something*, and Janet shouldn't even be thinking about becoming embroiled in the affair herself.

Clifford emerged from the radio room ten minutes later, looking wooden. Janet's head was bent diligently over a back-log of case notes and statistical data, but she turned from the work when it became clear that he wanted to speak to her.

'I'll have to go out to Diri Diri and . . .'

'Me too?' She was already on her feet, awash with the usual mixture of eagerness and dread at the thought of being with him, tinged with an extra ingredient of apprehensiveness because it was Diri Diri he was talking about.

'No, a nurse isn't needed. It's Frank Beddie. Remember his asthma problem? Stephanie says he's having a bad attack. He needs oxygen, and I'd like to try him on some different medication as well.' He named two preparations which were stronger than the Ventilin they had given Frank last time. 'But I can handle it myself.'

'You'd like me to find the drugs and sign them out?'

'Yes, please,' Clifford nodded. 'I'll tell Bill to get the plane ready. Frank's had bad attacks before, often in summer. Till now he hasn't needed hospital treatment, but this time . . . I don't know. Anyway, I may be out there for several hours while I assess his condition.'

Their eyes met briefly, then he slid away, almost guiltily. Could that be?

'Right . . .' Janet nodded.

She couldn't help feeling a wave of misery sweeping over her as she went to get the drugs Clifford had asked for. He was planning to spend several hours at Diri Diri, and he did not need a nurse. It didn't take much imagination to guess what that meant. Frank's attack was just the excuse for a rendezvous, and perhaps there had been other excuses of the kind over the past month and a half which Janet hadn't known about. Bill and Lance weren't gossips. If a couple of stops had been made at Diri Diri under Clifford's orders, would they necessarily have said anything about them? And Janet might well have been off-duty at the time.

It was not that she thought that Stephanie was inventing the story about Frank's asthma, but it was certainly an emergency call which Clifford wasn't going to hurry over.

Janet could not stop herself from picturing the scene at Diri Diri—Frank lying on the bed in his shaded bedroom, connected to an oxygen tank and monitoring equipment, perhaps under the influence of a drug which would take away the panic that could so often worsen an asthmatic's condition. Meanwhile, Stephanie and Clifford could be keeping a lover's tryst in some other part of the house or down by the river where Bill had swum that tense afternoon in December . . .

Oh, it was stupid, pointless torture to think these things. She did not love Clifford. She couldn't. He didn't deserve it. He wasn't worth the pain. It was an infatuation and she would soon squash it out of existence.

'Here you are.'

She dropped the packets of drugs into his hand and spoke coldly, wanting to put as much distance between them as she possibly could.

She could see that Clifford was a little startled by the snap in her tone and felt a perverse satisfaction. If he thought she didn't like him, so much the better. It was going to be—if it wasn't quite yet!—the truth. She let him go without the word of good wishes she usually gave to him or to Paul when they were going on a flight without her, and turned to Paul with unusual warmth when he arrived a few minutes later to take over Clifford's interrupted radio consultation session. At least with Paul she knew how she felt and where she stood . . .

Clifford did not return to Base until well after lunch. Paul had gone by this time, having been cheerful all morning and oblivious, as usual, of the finer shades of Janet's mood. For once, this was a sheer relief. When Clifford came in, Janet was still immersed in her statistics, but had almost finished the task.

'Tea?' Clifford asked as soon as he saw her, and went to put on the electric kettle.

He had given her no opportunity to ask about Frank Beddie's condition or to comment on the length of time he had spent at Diri Diri. 'Several hours' had been no exaggeration. She wouldn't have commented, of course, but he must have been afraid of it. The hasty, abstracted movements he was making, and the tuneless whistling, as he prepared the tea, were uncharacteristic.

He came to sit beside her when the hot yet refreshing drinks were ready, and pulled the papers she had been working on across in front of him.

'You've nearly finished.'

'Yes, although I should check it through with you.'

'Of course, but it looks as if you've done a good job. I'm pleased. Section Headquarters wants the report in as soon as possible, so why don't we check them through together now?'

'All right,' Janet replied. If he picked up on her reluctance, he didn't comment on it.

It took quite a long time to work through the statistics, which covered the number of patients attended, immunisations given and patients transported, as well as other details. Bill, Lance and Martin were writing up statistics of their own, too—number of transceiver sets in regular use, number of nautical miles and hours flown, number of landings made. It would all be collated as part of Benanda Base's annual report and sent to Sydney, where the Federal Council of the Service would include the figures in tables that covered the whole of Australia.

Recording the figures had been the kind of precise, practical task which Janet enjoyed as a variation on her normal work, but now she wished she had not volunteered to do it. It was bringing her into a proximity with Clifford that she very much did not want now, when she was trying so hard to reassess her feelings about him.

Of necessity, his head was bent very close to hers, and she wondered if, only an hour or two ago, Stephanie Beddie had been running her slim pale fingers through those thick dark waves of hair, while Frank was too ill and too pre-occupied with his fight for breath to know. Involuntarily, she shuddered away from Clifford.

'Are you all right?' he said.

'Yes, perfectly.'

'You don't seem happy today.'

'Oh? Why is that?' It was a stupid answer, Janet realised. She should simply have insisted that she was fine and got on with the work at hand.

'Just . . . I don't know. The set of your shoulders, the way you're frowning. I had a difficult time myself at Diri Diri, so perhaps I'm more attuned to it. Frank was quite ill, but didn't want to leave the station, and Stephanie was . . .'

'I'm not really interested, actually,' Janet interrupted frostily, trying to feel satisfied at his coldly surprised expression.

Had he really been planning to tell her about some lover's tiff, just like that, as if he had never kissed her, as if she was some kind of spinsterish confidante. Humiliation fought with anger inside her. Perhaps he really did think of her like that now.

'And I'm not unhappy,' she continued. 'You were wrong. I'm fine, and I'd like to get this work finished so I can go home, if you don't mind.'

'Janet, is there . . . ?'

'Please don't try to talk to me about your personal life as if we were friends. You and Stephanie—and Frank —have obviously got problems, but I don't particularly want to hear about them.'

He was silent for a long moment, then he turned back to the columns of figures and resumed the systematic checking with a calculator that he had been doing before, speaking each number aloud in a controlled monotone. For a long time, Janet fought against the urge to blurt out an apology, or a confession, but she managed to bite back the words, and eventually they had completed the shared task and she was free to go.

Janet lay on her bed thinking for a long time that afternoon, only roused from her reverie by Lorna calling her in to the evening meal. It was likely that she had thoroughly alienated Clifford now. Was she glad or sorry? She just didn't know. It would be sensible to be glad, to think with relief that this would certainly prevent any repetition of those dark moments of passion at Moollawindra six weeks ago, to tell herself that she had no illusions about Clifford now, but she couldn't quite do it. Clifford Ransome wasn't an easy man to hate in spite of everything.

Two weeks later, Janet had much recovered her equilibrium of spirit, and had somehow managed to find a perverse pleasure in the fact that she and Clifford virtually didn't speak to each other now, except when work strictly required it. She still ached dully in his presence, but felt safe, at least, from any further disturbance of her senses. He was never near enough to her to so much as brush her shoulder with an accidental hand, so she was spared the undermining effect of her physical awareness of him. At a distance, like this it was far easier to dislike him.

The fact that he seemed to be in communication with Diri Diri almost every day helped considerably as well. Even when Janet was at the Base during the morning radio session she never heard the calls. Significantly, the radio room door was shut when Clifford was talking to Stephanie, although this did not guarantee privacy for the pair, as anyone on the whole transceiver network might be listening.

Theirs was certainly an odd affair, Janet thought. Surely things would have to come to a head soon! What was Frank feeling? He couldn't be happy with the situation, could he?

One morning in early March, Janet was in the radio room when Diri Diri's transceiver set plugged in to the Flying Doctor frequency. The routine morning radio consultation had just finished and Paul, who had been dispensing advice this morning, had wheedled her into bringing him a cup of coffee. Martin had slipped down to the general store for some fruit juice, and would resume his place at the controls in ten minutes, to give out weather statistics, relay telegrammes, and pass on other information.

Janet had taken the opportunity to have a coffee break herself, after a steady session of work on case notes, and the discharge of a difficult patient who had spent the night in her care at the Base suffering mild concussion following a drunken fall outside the hotel. He had slept solidly through the night, so Janet had been able to rest for a few hours herself after checking his condition carefully, but she did feel a bit jaded and fuzzy, and it took her some time to recognise Frank Beddie's voice, disguised as it was by the urgency in his tone.

'Clifford?' He began abruptly.

'No, it's Paul Adams speaking,' Paul said, then gulped a hasty mouthful of coffee.

'Can you send a plane straight away? Absolutely straight away?'

'Where? What's wrong? Who is it?' Paul did not recognise the voice.

'Frank Beddie from Diri Diri,' Janet put in quickly.

'Frank?' Paul said sharply.

'Yes. It's Stephanie. She's . . . Just send Clifford up here straight away,' Frank said, his voice growing hoarse now and his breathing sounding tense and strained. 'And your nurse too.'

'But what's wrong? It'll help if we know . . .' Paul began, but Diri Diri's transceiver clicked out abruptly.

There was a moment of stunned silence while Paul and Janet stared at each other, their coffee forgotten.

'I'm the one on duty,' Paul said slowly. 'But Frank wants Clifford. In view of the fact that it's Stephanie, I suppose I'd better call him.'

'Do you think personal considerations should enter into it?' Janet flashed out before she could stop herself. It was a bitchy remark, and not like her. She caught Paul's surprised and quizzical stare and added quickly, 'Never mind. He'll have his beeper with him. I'll ring it straight away.'

They both anticipated the ring of the radio phone in response to the signal but it didn't come.

'He's not at home, then,' Paul said, finding his coffee and taking another absent-minded gulp. 'Perhaps you're right. It sounded urgent. If only he'd said more . . . I should go straight away.'

'Wait a minute,' Janet said. She didn't know why she was suddenly arguing against what she had said earlier. 'Just a minute or two.'

'I'll call Lance anyway,' Paul said. 'And if Clifford's not back by then, I will have to go . . .'

Janet nodded and Paul disappeared. Moments later there were footsteps on the wooden verandah and Clifford was in the room.

'I was just on my way out to the river when I was beeped,' he said. 'What's wrong?'

Their gaze met. It felt awkward, as it always did nowadays.

'An urgent call from Frank Beddie at Diri Diri,' Janet said, noting his instinctive flinch at the sound of the names. 'He asked for you.'

'What's wrong? His asthma?' Clifford took a step towards her, but she retreated automatically, shaking her head.

'No, not that. Something about Stephanie, but he wouldn't say. He sounded . . . very worried.'

Clifford's face had gone white to the lips, and even in the urgency of the moment, Janet could not help registering the fact with a sickening lurch of her heart. He loved Stephanie, and deeply. No doubt of that if he could look like that at the news that she was ill. Clifford had already moved towards the door that led out to the landing strip.

'Paul's gone to call Lance on the intercom. He was in the aircraft hangar . . .'

Clifford only nodded at this, and Janet had to almost run to keep up with him. In moments they were in the plane and Lance Norton, the sandy-haired second pilot who was on duty today, was starting the engine.

The flight seemed to drag on for hours, and for the first time, Janet found the drone of the engine and the crackle of the radio irritating and intrusive. From her position in the back, she was intensely aware of every impatient movement Clifford made. His body seemed wound like a spring and he stared out of the window, a hand tapping restlessly against the glass. It was clear that he was thinking the worst, and, though hating herself for

it, and not understanding at all how she could be feeling
such a thing, Janet sympathised with him.

Stephanie might be married to Frank, but that would
not lessen the pain Clifford was feeling if he really loved
her. Perhaps it would be for the best if, after this
drama—whatever it turned out to be—was safely over,
Frank and Stephanie were divorced and Clifford could
claim his love openly. As for herself, Janet knew that she
simply didn't enter the picture . . .

Janet had expected that Frank would be there, impatiently waiting at the airstrip when they touched
down, but the bare sweep of ground was deserted and
the only visible sign of life was one of the station
dogs going about its own canine business around the
outbuildings of the homestead.

Clifford and Janet left Lance at the plane, took a bag
of equipment each and began the two hundred yard walk
to the homestead. It was an unpleasant day. A wind was
blowing dust in from the north-west, and there was a
haze of low, dust-filled cloud sweeping in a slow curtain
across the sky. Diri Diri, in spite of the savage beauty of
its surroundings, and the relief of the belt of white-
trunked trees that marked the river, seemed a desolate
place today. 'A hundred miles from nowhere,' Janet
remembered Stephanie's words, not for the first time. A
place like this could be terrible if you were unhappy, if
you needed people, if something was wrong . . .

'Why is it so quiet? Has there been a mistake?' Janet
found herself saying.

She was speaking to Clifford's retreating back because
he was striding ahead rapidly. At her words he turned,
frowning, and flung a stinging reply back at her.

'Of course it isn't a mistake. The fact that there is no
one to meet us makes me doubly anxious. Can't you
walk faster?'

Janet felt as if she had been slapped. His demand was
unfair. The bag she carried was heavy and the air was
thick and soup-like. Every movement was an effort. But

she did manage to quicken her pace, goaded by his anger, and by the fact that he was now yards ahead of her.

The eerie desertion of Diri Diri was uninterrupted even as they crossed the baking yard towards the steps that led up to the verandah of the raised homestead building, but as their tread sounded on the wooden boards, a voice, hoarse and strained, came from somewhere inside.

'Is that you Frank?' Clifford called quickly.

'In the . . . bedroom.'

'He's having an asthma attack,' Janet said sharply as she recognised his laboured speech for what it was.

'Yes. That's why I've brought oxygen,' Clifford was still ahead of her, both in his walk and in his thoughts.

Janet bit her lip. Clifford knew Frank, knew his history and condition far better than she did, but she felt she should have thought sooner about the complication of his asthma nonetheless.

But she had no more time to worry about her relationship with Clifford, either personally or professionally. Blinds darkened the passage as they walked along it but hot light, strangely yellow and thick from the dust outside, flooded into the bedroom that Clifford turned into seconds later, and Janet gazed helplessly at what she saw there.

Frank, his face livid with fear and damp with sweat, supported Stephanie's tall slim form. She was wrapped only in a towel, the ends of her fair hair curling wet around her neck as though she had recently been in the bath. She was very unsteady on her feet and it was clear that Frank had been forcing her to pace around the room.

'Cliff!' Stephanie exclaimed with an unsteady and almost hysterical giggle.

He was at her side almost before the exclamation was out, but Janet still stood in the doorway, trying to regain her nursing instincts and stop the crawling of her spine at the sight of the rivulets of drying blood that had run from Stephanie's bare wrists and dripped on to the towel, on to her legs, and on to Frank's agitated body.

Everything was happening too quickly. Frank let go of Stephanie as Clifford took over the task of supporting her.

'You'll let me lie down, won't you, Cliff?' were the near-hysterical woman's words, said in a crazy, uncontrolled voice that slurred nearly every syllable.

'What have you taken, Stephanie?' Clifford asked urgently and sharply.

But Janet had no time to listen to the woman's reply. After releasing Stephanie, Frank had seemed to let go, as well, of the thin thread of determination that was holding him together. He was gasping for breath now, and showing clear signs of oxygen starvation.

'Where is your Ventilin?' she demanded.

'Bathroom.'

Janet was inside the small ensuite bathroom in a moment, and had little time to feel her stomach churn at the mess there—the bath, half-filled with rusty-pink water, and pools of it on the floor, a smashed water glass, a scatter of pills from two over-turned plastic bottles, a wet razor blade on the side of the bath, and an open bottle of brandy. Janet slipped across all this and reached into the open wall-cabinet. Yes, the Ventilin was there right in front of her, prominent at the front of the lower shelf, immediately ready for a severe asthmatic's urgent need.

But would Ventilin be enough? Frank inhaled rapidly three times, clearly desperate for breath now that Clifford was taking care of Stephanie and he had time to think of his own condition.

'It's . . . not working.'

Janet heard his rising panic and saw that he was finding speech almost impossible now. She flung a desperate glance at Clifford. He seemed fully occupied with Stephanie, and was questioning her in low, urgent tones, but he must have caught Janet's movement as he made a concise reply, apparently without even needing to look at Frank.

'Hydrocortisone, 200 mils. In the bag you brought in.'

'And then we'll be going to Broken Hill?' She wanted to have time to work out exactly what she needed to do before they made the trip, but to her intense surprise, he was shaking his head.

'We won't be going to Broken Hill now. It's not . . . advisable.'

'But . . .'

'Broken Hill? No!' Stephanie had snapped out of her drugged state for a moment and frozen at the words. 'I won't go there! I'll stay here . . . even if I die!'

'It's all right, Stephanie. We won't go to Broken Hill. Just come with me and we'll sit down calmly in the lounge-room,' Clifford said to her, soothing and concerned.

He began to lead her from the room, leaving Janet dumb with amazement. From what she had seen in the bathroom, it was quite clear that Stephanie had over-dosed not only on tablets of some kind but on alcohol as well. She needed gastric lavage, careful monitoring . . . Frank had had to keep her marching on her feet so she would stay conscious. Frank himself was now in a serious condition which might well warrant hospitalisation, and Clifford was coolly saying that both patients would be treated here.

Janet's mind raced as she prepared Frank's hydrocor-tisone injection, and she had to use all her professional will to concentrate on getting the exact dose and re-membering all the procedures involved in the task. Hot anger was replacing her amazement now as she began to realise exactly what was going on.

Stephanie didn't want to go to hospital, neither did Frank, and Clifford agreed—and it wasn't for medical reasons.

He was back in the room now, taking something from

his own bag of equipment. Janet didn't bother to see what it was, but followed him from the room again.

'You can't do this!' She controlled her bubbling fury with difficulty. Janet was a quiet girl, and an even-tempered one, but if there was something which could arouse her anger, it was this—the disregard of professional ethics.

'Do what?' His question was testy, impatient. He did not even look guilty or ashamed. Janet felt a whole world of emotion crumbling within her. She had at least trusted his medical morals until now. But how wrong she must have been! And where did that leave her painful love for him? Had she been in love with an illusion all along?

'Those two need hospital treatment, both of them,' she burst out.

'On the contrary. They can both be treated here. Now I suggest you . . .'

'I don't believe you're saying this.' Janet was speaking as quietly as she could, aware of Frank's worsening state close by in the bedroom, but she saw Clifford's warning frown and managed to lower her voice, speaking in a desperate whisper now. 'You can't jeopardise the lives of two people because you're tied up in some revolting kind of triangle with them. It's against everything medicine stands for. It doesn't matter how much gossip there is about what's happening here today, how much your name is dragged through the mud because you're personally involved, you've got to do the right thing!'

Clifford took in a sharp breath and Janet saw that she had caught him on the raw. His eyes narrowed and glittered, and she waited for an admission that she was right, and his instructions for a change of plan. They didn't come.

'We'll talk about this later,' he said. 'Right now there isn't time. Give that injection immediately, please, and then put him on oxygen. When you're satisfied with his condition, come and see me.'

There was no arguing with that whiplash tone, in spite
of her violent disagreement and outrage. Janet turned
on her heel, realising as she looked down at the syringe
in her hand, that she was trembling. But in seconds she
was in control, confronted by Frank's worsening state.
Without another wasted moment—guiltily she realised
that her outburst to Clifford had wasted too many
already—she swabbed Frank's arm with antiseptic and
gave the injection, then set up the oxygen equipment,
still not daring to believe that Frank would be all right.

She realised that she felt very afraid, and needed the
reassurance of a big city hospital, with its specialists
always on call, its high-technology equipment only a
short trolley journey away, its well-oiled procedures for
every emergency. Diri Diri was so lonely, her own
responsibility so great. No wonder Stephanie felt
stranded here in this isolation that was such a contrast to
her city background . . .

Many tense minutes later, when it became clear that
Frank was going to win his fight for breath, Janet could
begin to come to herself. His cyanosed appearance had
gone, his pulse rate had fallen, and he was far more
relaxed. He was a strong man, well-built and tall. Janet
had never really studied him before but she did so now.
If it wasn't for the asthma which handicapped him, he
would be a very capable and powerful man, and Janet
thought that he had probably worked on his physique
consciously, to minimise the effect that his asthma had
on his life and work. It was amazing how much he had
recovered his strength and composure already. He
smiled at her faintly, and lifted the oxygen mask for a
moment to speak.

'That's good,' he said. 'I'm okay now. But . . . go and
see if the doctor needs help with Stephanie.'

'He loves her. It's going to be hard—and unfair—for
him to lose her to Clifford,' Janet thought suddenly.
Aloud she said: 'I'm going to, but when I've checked
your pulse once more.'

She tried to dismiss the tumult of feeling within her as she thought of the other emergency. It seemed Clifford had been right about Frank. Hospital wouldn't be necessary. But what about Stephanie? How could Clifford be taking such a risk?

It was horribly quiet in the shaded lounge-room. Stephanie lay there on the couch, her face pale, her eyes closed. Clifford was sponging the last of the blood from her wrists, which were now bandaged and looked thin and frail. Janet's heart leapt into her mouth.

'What's happened? Why is she . . . ?'

'She's asleep, Janet,' Clifford said, brief and cold. 'And I don't want her woken.'

'But . . . I don't understand. All those tablets, the loss of blood, the brandy . . .'

'A good deal of it was an act,' he explained crisply. 'Which is the reason I was not as concerned as you . . . suggested I should have been. Haven't you heard of the "cry for help" syndrome?'

'Of course I have, but . . .'

'She'd slashed the razor across lightly a couple of times—and as you must know, it's a lengthwise cut that does real damage—and she's let the blood run prettily for a bit, but the wounds were already closed by coagulation when we arrived. As for the tablets and the alcohol, she'd taken a few Valiums and two Mandrax. The brandy she had scarcely touched. I gave her a good dose of ipecac and it all came up again. The whole escapade tired her rather, and she's sleeping it off. Satisfied?'

The deliberate barb goaded Janet into a rash reply.

'No, I'm not satisfied. You only had her word about what she'd taken.'

'Not quite true. There are certain signs and symptoms which give a guide.'

'An inexact one . . .'

'And anyway, as you have pointed out so plainly, Stephanie and I know each other rather well,' he went on silkily. 'I knew she was play-acting.'

'How could you be so sure?'

For a moment he hesitated, then:

'Because it's happened before.' He saw her gasp and looked satisfied.

'Here at Diri Diri?'

'Yes. Last October,' he said, his face a mask. 'Stephanie . . . became depressed and made a half-hearted attempt at ending it all. Like this one, she soon admitted that she didn't want it to succeed.'

'But shouldn't she have been put in hospital for observation in any case?' Janet said, still wanting to fight him every inch of the way. 'Shouldn't she still be? She might try it again . . .'

'I don't think so,' he said. 'She's already ashamed of it. In fact, she begged me not to even put this affair on record. But as far as hosp . . .'

'Exactly!' Janet cut him off unashamedly, in bitter triumph. 'My accusation stands. You care more about keeping yourself and Stephanie out of the gossip than about your patient's well-being and your duty as a doctor, and I . . .'

'That's enough!' There was a dangerous note in his voice which Janet had never heard before and which was as hard as diamond. 'You've had your say. If you're serious about these accusations, why not make a written complaint?'

'I will! I'll do exactly that!'

'But for now, there's some cleaning up to do. When everything's settled, we'll be on our way.'

Janet found that there was nothing left to say, although anger and humiliation as well as a hurt that she would not fully admit to—still coursed through her. She thought of the mess in the bathroom. She would get that out of the way. It was unhygienic and dangerous, and the cool little room and the practical task would both be refuges, in their different ways, from Clifford and his anger.

She stepped forward, expecting that he would move

aside for her, but she must have taken him by surprise as
he didn't move and she bumped against his torso. Both
their arms came out defensively and Janet felt the warm
touch of his fingers on her bare arms, and saw the faint
dew of sweat on his tanned throat and collarbone. A
shudder of longing rippled through her and she wanted
desperately to wind her arms around him and bury her
face in his shoulder, confessing the real underlying reason for her anger and hearing an answering
confession from him.

For a moment her hands had tightened against his
waist involuntarily, and she almost thought that his
fingers gripped her arms too, then he gave a rasping sigh
and stepped back abruptly to let her pass. It had been a
moment of contact that she could have done without.

She went in search of cleaning things and found them
in a cupboard in the big homestead kitchen. The kitchen
was untidy and not very clean, and it seemed as if
Stephanie had become disenchanted with housekeeping
in this isolated place.

When Janet returned to the bathroom, she saw that
Frank was still taking in oxygen, but he was lying calmly,
and with his eyes closed, so she guessed that Clifford
must have told him that Stephanie's condition was now
stable and safe. She went quietly past without disturbing
him and began her work, seeing the scene much more
rationally now that she knew Stephanie had been ex-
aggerating her condition. Yes, in that, at least, she had
to admit that Clifford had been right.

The scattering of pills and the broken glass, the pink
stain of the water—it was all a bit *too* dramatic. If
Stephanie had really wanted to die, she would have gone
about it much less flamboyantly. Clearly, it was a call to
somebody for rescue.

To Frank? Or was it to Clifford?

'That's good enough, Janet.'

Clifford's voice startled her some minutes later, and
she scrambled to her feet, afraid of him now in a way she

had never been before. She sensed that he had not
forgotten or forgiven her accusations and would not do
so for some time. Was she prepared to back them up
with a written complaint as he had suggested? Out of
defiance and bravado she had said she would, but that
was in the heat of the moment and now she felt far less
sure.

'I'll have to leave Benanda,' she thought wildly. 'I
can't stay now.'

'We'll get going as soon as we can,' Clifford was
saying, very cool.

'I've taken the equipment back. I'd like you to go out
to the plane now and prepare a stretcher for Stephanie
and oxygen gear for Frank.'

'But I thought . . .'

'It was you who assumed they weren't coming in for
observation,' he interrupted smoothly. 'You were jumping to conclusions. I always intended that they should
both go to Broken Hill, but I wanted to wait until
things were calmer. It's the emotional crisis I'm more
concerned with, not the physical one, and now that
Stephanie is herself again, she has agreed to go.'

Janet found that there was nothing to say. Clifford had
all the answers now. Was he enjoying seeing her so
wretched? It couldn't be that he had guessed the awful
secret of her unwilling love for him, could it? He was a
very perceptive man. That had been proved quite clearly
this afternoon . . .

The journey to Broken Hill was a very quiet one.
Lance was less talkative even than Bill, Clifford was
locked in brooding thoughts of his own, and Stephanie
was asleep. Clifford had judged it wise—and safe—to
give her a mild sedative, and Frank was still weak and
weary after his tiring attack.

Janet was very happy not to speak, although it gave
her far too much time for thoughts.

Diri Diri had been left in the hands of the head
stockman who had returned from a distant paddock with

three other station workers just as Frank and Stephanie had been taken onto the plane. The two would stay in Broken Hill for several days—as much to sort out their lives as to recover their health. That fact was not spoken but Janet knew that it was understood by everyone. She felt certain of the outcome of the sorting out, too. Frank would stay on at Diri Diri, while Stephanie would go south to be joined by Clifford as soon as he could be replaced at Benanda Base.

It was late afternoon when the Piper Chieftain finally taxied to rest at the Base after the flight to Broken Hill. Lance ducked quickly away to the air-craft hangar. Janet herself was about to leave, too, but . . .

'And now, Janet, I think you and I had better have a talk,' Clifford said.

CHAPTER NINE

JANET had not been inside Clifford Ransome's tranquil plant-filled house since the night of her arrival in Benanda. That was over three months ago, but it somehow seemed much longer.

He ushered her, without speaking, to the same seat on the screened-in verandah that she had occupied that first night, and when, finally, he did speak it was only to ask a laconic question.

'Something to drink?'

'An orange juice . . .'

'You can have something stronger.' He summoned a faint smile. 'The sun's well over the yardarm.'

'Actually . . .'

'I'm having a brandy-and-dry.'

'All right then.' History seemed to be repeating itself, for what it was worth.

Clifford returned with the drinks a few minutes later and sat down. Janet stared at the frosted glass in her hand, waiting for him to speak and feeling like a schoolgirl sent up to see the Head. She was in for a reprimand, perhaps even notice of dismissal. She didn't think she deserved it, but wouldn't it be easier in the long run if she did have to leave? Perhaps that was what Clifford was thinking . . .

'I'm going to try to explain to you about myself and Stephanie Beddie.'

His words, when they came after a continuing pause, surprised her. It wasn't the tone—that, as expected, was very cool. But she hadn't anticipated an explanation of any kind. And did she really want one? No! She understood everything very well.

'There's no need,' she said quickly and sharply. 'It's of

no importance to me.' She did not realise it, but she looked very compact, firm and contained.

'I see.' Clifford hesitated, then continued. 'Somehow I thought it might have been.'

He smiled thinly and Janet flinched under the certainty that he knew the secret of her mixed up feelings about him. It was the kind of exposure that her private soul hated. Rashly, in a doomed effort to preserve her sense of self-worth, she attempted a retort.

'Then you flattered yourself, I'm afraid.' Her chin was lifted but the self-assurance was only a performance. 'I have no interest in your . . . affairs.'

'So am I to take it that this talk is for nothing?' he queried.

'No,' Janet said, still business-like and composed. 'I'm glad of it. Because I'd like to apologise— for questioning your decisions openly like that, and in an emergency.'

'For questioning openly and in an emergency, but not for thinking it privately, perhaps?' he probed lightly, seeming unmoved by her apology.

'I don't have to answer that . . .'

'No, you don't. I can draw my own conclusions.'

'Very well. Think what you like.'

There was a small silence. Janet became aware that the light was beginning to fade. It was growing dark earlier these days. The hot weather would finish soon. Perhaps then her feelings would be easier to keep in perspective. But Clifford was continuing now.

'Your comments today were . . . unfortunate. Unfortunate and inappropriate. I'd rather forget that they were ever said, and I'll try not to let it affect our working relationship, but if you do want to pursue the matter formally . . .'

'I don't,' Janet said hastily. She met his gaze and flushed at its penetration.

'I'm glad,' he said. 'I wouldn't like to think that we could actually . . . be enemies. Are we enemies, Janet?'

'No.'

But what were they? Janet wondered miserably as she finished her drink in silence. Certainly not friends. What was left? An uneasy neutrality that was very unnatural to her. And when her heart—still, in spite of everything —cried out for so much more.

She was on the point of rising to leave with a murmured excuse when Clifford spoke again.

'To seal the bargain, how about a swim and a picnic tea?'

'I'd rather not,' Janet blurted out. 'I mean, Lorna will be expecting me.'

And you're only asking out of duty and politeness, she could have added. Can't you see how strained the evening would be? This talk hasn't eased anything between us. Why are you forcing the issue?

He did not betray any disappointment, only a faint, politely concealed surprise. He must have expected that she would have jumped at the chance to be with him. So he definitely knew her secret! How miserable!

It would have been easy and natural to leave then, but before she could do so, a car pulled to a gravelly halt in the front yard, a door banged, and clattering footsteps came up the wooden verandah steps. It was Marcia Fairfax. Her energetic and imperious knock sounded loudly, and she was clearly in an impatient mood.

'Clifford! Oh, hullo Janet—I did it! Or at least, *we* did it! I got into the fashion course in Sydney, the mid-year intake, and I'd never have done it if you hadn't given me all that help with the presentation of my application! You are a darling!'

She threw her arms round his neck and gave him a frank, childish kiss, and in that moment, Janet saw that she had been mistaken all along about Clifford's relationship with the exuberant and discontented elder daughter of Fairwater Park.

Marcia had had a crush on Clifford, probably, but had recognised it as one herself, and had her eyes too firmly on a career in the city to care about a long-term relationship at this time in her life. As for Clifford, he had probably enjoyed the role of mentor, and had given some very practical help to his younger friend, it now appeared. Oh, perhaps there had been more to it—a few mild kisses, some dalliance and flirtation, but it certainly didn't seem now like the sinister two-timing Janet had believed it to be. No wonder Marcia hadn't seemed to mind about Stephanie Beddie.

'Are you off, Janet?' Clifford broke off from his enthusiastic but almost fatherly congratulations to ask the question.

'Yes, I'd better. I'm feeling quite tired,' she nodded. 'Congratulations Marcia.'

'Thanks. I'm feeling absolutely thrilled.'

'So you should be.'

Janet got herself away. The day had been a difficult one, and if anything she was only feeling worse about Clifford than ever.

Paul Adams dropped round that night after the evening meal. It was unexpected. He had not been seeking her out lately, and Janet did not particularly want to see him. Lorna was out, spending the evening at Fairwater Park with Gloria Fairfax, who was quite a good friend, so Janet entertained Paul with cool drinks and music on the back verandah.

He wanted to know about the emergency at Diri Diri, of course, so Janet told him, leaving all spice out of the account. He complained about it in his usual light way.

'You don't even seem interested,' he said. 'Don't you realise that what goes on there is this season's juiciest gossip at Benanda?'

'Yes, I do realise,' Janet retorted—too sharply.

'Hey sorry!' Paul said, then added teasingly, 'don't tell me you're in love with Frank!'

Janet contrasted Frank's beefy, country-style good looks with Clifford's lean frame and compassionate eyes.

'No, I'm not in love with Frank.'

'Just a joke.'

'I know . . . I'm not being much fun tonight.'

'Don't worry about it. I daresay today was pretty tiring. I wish those two would make up their minds to run off together. Stephanie needs more people and excitement around. If you ask me that's the reason behind her breakdowns more than pining after Clifford. They aren't really suited, but if that's what they want, why don't they do something about it and leave poor old Frank to run Diri Diri and reconstruct his life in peace?' Paul said.

'Is everyone really so certain that that's what's in the wind?' Janet asked. She knew quite well what the answer would be, but wanted to torture herself by hearing it anyway, to wipe out the stupid little spark of hope that would keep glowing in spite of everything.

'Well, there's no lack of evidence,' Paul was saying. 'She and Clifford knew each other in Sydney before Frank ever came on to the scene. I think they were even engaged. Then Frank came into the picture. He was in the city doing a business management course to improve his running of the station. Stephanie fell for those blue eyes and outback muscles and tan—and probably the glamour of a prosperous big cattle station got to her, too. Clifford followed her up here, and was on hand when she realised she'd made a mistake. I don't know why he didn't spirit her off months ago.'

'Yes, it does seem surprising,' Janet murmured, trying to keep the misery out of her voice. 'Since it all sounds so cut and dried.'

'Something is bound to happen now,' Paul went on cheerfully. 'Maybe Frank'll step aside gracefully, or Clifford will get the impetus to force the issue. I must say, he doesn't seem to have much push about the whole thing. Hanging around here waiting for Stephanie to lift her little finger.'

'It might not be like that,' Janet said quickly—why on earth was she defending him like this?

'No, I suppose not. Maybe he's changed his mind. Maybe he's here for other reasons altogether, but I don't see how.'

'You're here,' Janet pointed out.

'Aha! But in fact that's why I came round tonight, to tell you my news,' he said. 'I'm not going to be here much longer.'

'You've resigned!'

'More than that. I've got a job to go to at the Prince of Wales in Sydney. A step up the ladder, too.'

'That's terrific, Paul!'

'No need to ask if you'll miss me. I can see that you won't,' Paul said flippantly.

'Oh Paul, it's not that . . .' Janet began.

'I know. You're pleased for me,' he nodded. 'We mucked up any chance of an affair—or even a good friendship—long ago, didn't we? And don't worry, I'm not carrying a torch for you.'

'I didn't think you were.'

'What about you, anyway? How long are you going to be content in this town?' Paul asked the question searchingly. He was clearly in the mood for probing deeper feelings tonight.

'I . . . I don't know,' Janet said. 'I love it, in lots of ways . . .'

'And yet, isn't there something missing? What about romance? You're not the kind of girl to want to stay single forever. It's a difficult life for a single person, and there's no one here for you.'

'There's Pat Jackson,' Janet said, more outspoken about her feelings than usual.

'Are you serious?'

'Not really,' she admitted. 'I like him, but . . .'

'He's not right for you,' Paul finished for her authoritatively.

'You've really got Benanda's couples worked out, haven't you? You know exactly who's right for who and who isn't!'

Janet spoke flippantly, realising as she did so why she had brought Pat Jackson's name into the conversation so unnecessarily. 'There's no one here for you,' Paul had said, and she had thought of Clifford straight away. Not for her. Of course he wasn't. He never had been. But that was too hard to think about right now, so she had seized on the safer image of Pat Jackson. Someone who seemed to want her, even if she didn't want him in the same way . . .

Paul went away about half an hour later, after enthusing in more detail over his new job. He was to leave in six weeks, and his departure *would* leave a gap. Even though their relationship had been at times a messy and uncomfortable one, as he himself had acknowledged, Janet would miss him. No replacement had been found yet, of course. In fact, Clifford didn't even know of the new development, but an advertisement would go out very soon.

'Perhaps a woman would be nice,' Janet found herself thinking.

She expected something to happen over the next few days, following Paul's information about Stephanie and Clifford's past, and his opinion about the inevitability of Stephanie's marriage breaking up. What would it be? She steeled herself for an announcement from Clifford that he, too, was leaving Benanda, or that Stephanie would be moving into the quiet house beside the Base.

But nothing happened. It was disquieting, and she found it a struggle to give her usual undiluted care to the work of nursing. She was sent on several emergency flights—each time, to her great relief, with Paul. There was a pair of children who had been severely stung by a swarm of bees, a stockman whose leg had been crushed against a fence by an angry bull, and what turned out to be a minor accident at the Tanama gasfields.

Now that Paul was leaving, Janet found that they could re-establish some of their initial light-hearted camaraderie, but that wasn't really enough to cover her feelings about Clifford. If only she knew exactly what was happening, perhaps she could accept it, but until she knew, she couldn't keep her naive and foolish heart from insisting that there must be a mistake somewhere. If she could feel like this, he *must* be feeling something too.

It was over a week after the dramatic events at Diri Diri when she ventured to ask Clifford about Frank and Stephanie, realising that it would seem very unnatural if she *didn't* ask about her patients' progress at Broken Hill.

'You've missed their news on the transceiver, then?' he said when she finally mentioned it over morning coffee.

'Yes, I . . . don't seem to have been around during the radio sessions.'

Of course she could not tell him that she had deliberately avoided them because *he* was almost always there, sitting beside Martin Baird at the controls, dispensing advice in his usual calm, reassuring way, his lean fingers wrapped around a tea cup, or scribbling something rapidly with a pen . . .

'And anyway, if I'm to go by what you said to me before, you're not particularly concerned about Stephanie and Frank Beddie, one way or another . . . ?' he was saying. It was part statement, part question. Was he criticising her lack of involvement as a nurse?

'Of course I'm concerned about them as patients, but . . .'

'That wasn't an attack, Janet.' He looked at her quizzically.

'I'm sorry.'

'They're still in Broken Hill,' was his reply to her initial question now.

'Still in the hospital?' She was surprised.

'In a motel,' he explained. 'But they're going in for some counselling. They've got a few problems. Of course you've gathered that.'

'Yes,' she nodded tightly. 'It's common knowledge, isn't it? I hope it all works out . . . and that you get what you want.'

Do I mean that sincerely? she thought. No . . . not if what you want is Stephanie, and I know it is. She turned away from him and went to the sink, so that he couldn't see the sudden pointless tears that blinded her, and didn't notice the surprised, searching look he flung in her direction.

It was inevitable, of course, that they should have to fly together again soon, but Janet's heart sank and she felt the muscles of her temples tighten a few days later as she heard his voice over the phone in her little flat.

'Paul's already on a flight,' he said, as if apologising for the fact that they would be teamed together. 'This one is an unusual one—but I'll tell you about it when you get here. You'll be on that bike, I suppose?'

'Yes.'

'Watch out for semi-trailers!'

He rang off before she could reply to the first light-hearted comment he had made to her in what seemed like—and probably was!—weeks. She wished he hadn't reminded her of that day, because it made her think, instantly, of his fingers in her hair.

'Have a cup of tea and I'll fill you in before we leave,' he said when she arrived, neater and fresher in her uniform after the ride across town now that the weather wasn't quite so scorching.

Clifford seemed more relaxed today than he had been for a long time. Was that the change in the weather too? There was an abstracted anxiety and underlying tension that was gone from his manner now. With a cold pang Janet realised what it probably meant—Stephanie had made the decision to leave Frank, and Clifford could look forward to a definite future with her.

He was making the tea himself moving with brisk energy and confidence, a half-smile breaking over his face every now and then, although he seemed unaware of it. Wasn't that just the way a man like Clifford would look if he was truly in love and if the course of that love at last looked as though it was going to run smoothly?

'Aren't we in a hurry?' Janet asked a little crisply, as she saw him shake some biscuits from a packet onto a plate. He glanced at her and his smile faded.

'This is an important case,' he replied, more stiffly now. 'But not an urgent one. Didn't I say that I wanted to talk to you about it before we left?'

'Yes, you did, but . . .'

'Then leave the decisions to me.'

'I'm sorry.'

They did not speak until he was seated near her with the tea and Janet couldn't help feeling guiltily aware that she had been the one to spoil his mood. Perhaps she should ask him straight out about his plans for Stephanie and himself, stop pretending as she had been doing that she had no interest in it. It would give away the secret of her love completely, of course, if Clifford was not fully aware of it already, but wouldn't anything be better than this sense of foreboding anticipation which was filling her these days?

She was on the point of saying something when Clifford himself began to speak.

'We'll be going up to a place called Pitchiwatana Bore,' he said. 'It's a very isolated station with quite a high aboriginal population, many of whom come and go and still keep up a lot of their old hunting traditions, and that sort of thing. An old woman has walked into the station with two children who seemed to be malnourished.'

'An *old* woman?' Janet put in.

'Yes, apparently the children's great-grandmother. The grandmother is dead, and the mother—who was very young—had gone off to the city. This old woman had been looking after the kids very well on the station, with help from younger people in the black community,

but a few months ago she decided to . . . go walkabout
—I wish there was a better phrase for it,' Clifford broke
off and frowned.

'I know what you mean,' Janet nodded. 'That one
oversimplifies and demeans their nomadic life-style
somehow, doesn't it? Or at least, some people use the
expression that way.'

She was listening intently to Clifford's words now,
leaning forward, her hands gripping the mug of tea she
held. She had almost forgotten that this was Clifford,
and that minutes ago she had been feeling so terrible
about him. He was leaning forward too, and when their
eyes met—both concerned and engrossed—it was
suddenly quite easy to smile at him.

'Anyway . . .' He broke the moment, sitting back in
his chair again, leaving Janet bereft of his nearness. 'She
went off into the bush with the two kids a few months ago
and she's just turned up again. Probably a few years ago
in a good season like this she could have fed them well
enough with her knowledge of desert food, but now . . .
she's too old.'

'So we're to pick up the children and check them over
and take them to hospital?' Janet asked.

'It's a little more complicated than that, I'm afraid,'
Clifford said. 'Otherwise I might have gone without a
nurse. No, the real problem is the old woman's attitude.
She's reliving some of the old tribal kinship and ritual
taboos. I spoke to one of the younger men over the
transceiver. He was taught a lot about the old ways by his
grandfather, and apparently she's got them a bit mixed
up. The upshot of it is that she'll only hand those
children over to a woman, and not a woman from her
own tribe.'

'To a white woman, though?'

'We don't know.'

'Poor old thing,' Janet said. 'It'll be very hard for her.
It's obvious that it's the children she cares about, doing
her duty by the mother and the family, and she just

doesn't realise that she's too old to look after them properly.'

'If she doesn't give them to you, we'll have to take them away by force in the end, of course,' Clifford said.

'Oh!'

'Our last resort, Janet.'

'I hope it won't come to that.' She was suddenly determined that it wouldn't, that she'd find a way to take the children gently. It was for this kind of thing that she had come to the desert, but she knew that her need to prove herself to Clifford again and again was part of it, too. 'How is her English?'

'She used to speak it quite well, apparently,' Clifford said. 'But she's using her mother tongue more and more now. There's a younger woman there who she has trusted in the past and who'll be able to interpret for you if necessary.'

They left soon after. Janet was glad that Clifford had prepared her with the long explanation, and that she had the whole of the plane journey to think about what she might say, to the old woman. Inevitably, memories came back of her childhood at Moollawindra. She and Tony and Catherine had played very freely with several black children on the property, and had felt completely at ease with them. As an adult, of course, it wasn't so easy. She was much more aware of differences in culture, circumstances, outlook, but perhaps her past would help her to overcome these . . .

Once they had touched down at Pitchiwatana Bore, no time was wasted. An aboriginal stockman picked them up at the airstrip and drove them not to the main homestead, but to the more make-shift-looking aboriginal settlement down near the trees that marked the wide dry creek bed.

There was an expectant and uneasy feeling in the air when Janet got out of the vehicle. Clifford stayed behind —being male as well as white, he would only cause the old woman more alarm and fear. But he had briefed

Janet thoroughly about what he wanted her to do—the observations he would have made himself on both the children and the great-grandmother.

The unusual trio had camped themselves away from the other dwellings, right by the creek beneath a tree. Alice William, the woman who would interpret for Janet if needed, showed her the way.

'She's very sick,' Alice explained, obviously concerned and saddened. 'She can hardly see at all now, either. Don't upset her—or try, won't you?'

'Of course,' Janet said. 'But we have to think of the children . . .'

'Meena?' Alice called quietly as they approached.

'Meena!' Janet exclaimed. Alice turned in surprise.

'What's the matter?'

'Did she, and her son, used to live at Moollawindra Station, up further north? He was a stockman, and she . . .'

'Yes, for about five years. But how did you know?'

'I lived there myself.'

'One of the Greens?'

'Yes,' Janet nodded.

'She won't remember you.' For a minute Alice William's face had brightened, but now it fell again.

'You never know,' Janet said. 'Old people's memories can be very patchy. You think it's a blank, and then suddenly they'll surprise you with something very clear.'

They had reached the patch of shade where the old woman and the two children sat. Meena had her back to the settlement from which they had come, as if rejecting it mistrustfully, and she was staring out towards the horizon through the ghost gums. The two children—small for their ages of three and four—lay listlessly. One was beside Meena, and one in her lap . . .

Janet was down at the creek for over an hour. It was a very quiet hour, and progress in communicating with Meena was very slow. Alice was right. The old woman showed no memory of Moollawindra at all, let alone of

Janet, and she refused to speak English, talking creakily and shakily in her own native tongue instead.

First she insisted that she wanted a bag of flour and one of powdered milk and would go off with the children again, but then she seemed to change her mind and said she would stay if her son brought food for them. Since her son was living on a property over two hundred miles away, this didn't help.

As they talked, Janet managed to examine the children. They had the distended stomachs and listless attitude of malnourished children, but they responded quite well when she tried to play with them, and she guessed that with care and an improvement in diet made gradually to accustom their systems to richer foods, they could be restored to full health.

'It's getting nowhere,' Alice said eventually. 'She just nods to everything, except when I say the children should be taken away, then she shakes her head and —well, you saw how she caught hold of little Jacky then.'

'May I try talking to her again?' Janet asked. 'Perhaps speaking English will force her to think in the present more.'

She began to speak, not quite knowing what she was going to say at first. She asked Meena about her life, refusing to be put off by the lack of response, told about her own, asked Meena about her health. She mentioned Moollawindra again, and this time was rewarded by a faint flash of recognition in the old woman's eyes.

'I'm Janet Green. Do you remember me?'

But the half-blind eyes were dull and uninterested again.

'What about my mother and father? Donald and Maggie Green. Mrs Maggie. You used to work in the kitchen sometimes with Mrs Maggie.'

'Yes I did! She was a nice lady!' Suddenly this surprising consciousness.

'But you were much younger then,' Janet went on.

'You're getting very old now. You knew me when I was a little girl, but I'm grown up now, as you can see.'

'Yes . . .'

Janet caught Alice's nod of approval as she realised where the conversation was going . . .

Half an hour later it was over. The old woman had lapsed into forgetfulness again, saying, 'Jacky, Susie, you go with Mrs Maggie up to the big house,' and clearly thinking she was back at Moollawindra, but at least she had let them go willingly, and Alice would stay with her by the creek, bringing her tea and bread and trying to persuade her to come up to the homestead where she could be properly looked after, without being forced to make many changes in her way of life.

Janet walked slowly back up to the landrover where Clifford still sat, the passenger door open and his long legs dangling out of the vehicle. He was on his feet as soon as he saw them, and coming their way, taking the smaller child out of Janet's arms.

'Janet, you're a miracle!' He was laughing in triumph, and before she could step away he had squeezed her with his free arm and planted a kiss squarely on her forehead.

It wasn't what she wanted right now—a reminder of how much a caress from him meant to her, and how little it meant to him. But the moment was over almost at once and his attention was completely focussed on the two children.

A bag of instruments had been brought from the plane and he had them arranged in the back of the vehicle already. In ten minutes, each child's condition had been checked as thoroughly as possible in the difficult circumstances, with Janet standing by to help Clifford, holding the children's attention and adding her own observations.

'We'll take them to Charleville,' Clifford decided finally. 'It's closer by road to this place than Broken Hill, and if Alice, as you said, has decided to add them to her own family . . .'

'She seemed pretty definite,' Janet said.

'I'm glad. I'd hate to see them fostered out in the city. They'll only need a couple of weeks of hospitalisation, and then I think you'll prove to be right, Janet. No permanent damage.'

There was an awkward pause. A goodly scattering of people were gathered round to hear the news and they were all talking now in pairs or groups. If Janet had been friends with Clifford—not painfully and hopelessly in love with him—she might have hugged him right now. In his cream pants and soft denim-blue shirt, his familiar body looked so inviting and safe, and the long emotional talk with Meena had not been easy. It had left Janet drained . . .

For a moment she found that she was swaying towards him, suddenly weak, but he had not seen––thank goodness!—and stepped aside, speaking casually.

'How did you do it, Janet? Anything special? Or was it mainly Alice? When you were down there for so long, I began to be sure you had failed.'

'I knew Meena,' Janet said. 'That helped. I remembered her from Moollawindra. Her son was a stockman there. She thought I was my mother—"Mrs Maggie". We talked about time passing, growing old . . .'

'Janet, this must have proved to you, as it has to me although I knew it already, what an asset you are to the Benanda team.' Suddenly he was very serious, and speaking in a low tone so that no one else would hear. 'Paul's leaving. The future is . . . very up in the air. But I hope you'll stay. You will, won't you?'

'I . . . I don't know.'

What was he saying? Why was the future so up in the air? Just because of Paul? No . . . It was Stephanie Clifford was thinking about. When he asked Janet if she was planning to stay, it was the region and its people he was thinking of, people like the ones who surrounded them now, not himself, not his own needs. Or her own.

Suddenly Janet's success that morning tasted

sour. Would such things matter nearly so much to her when Clifford was gone, when she didn't have the satisfaction—a poor substitute for love, but satisfaction nonetheless—of working with him as a team and gaining his approval and respect.

'We should get going, shouldn't we?' he said briefly.

CHAPTER TEN

HOME to Benanda! Janet's room beckoned as a refuge from Clifford's torturing presence, and she couldn't wait for the flight back from Charleville to be over. The two bewildered but quiet children had been handed safely over to a nurse at the hospital, who had seemed both capable and genuinely concerned. Alice William and her husband would be able to make the long drive to Charleville in about a week, and would stay there with the children until they were ready to come home. Clifford would be in touch with Charleville medical staff about their progress. Meena was to be left at Pitchiwatana. In fact, her health was deteriorating badly, and in other circumstances Clifford might have wanted her put in hospital, but in this case, Meena would only be unhappy and distressed.

'It's better for her to live out her life in a place where she's happy,' Clifford had said quietly to Janet, and she had agreed.

All this meant that, to all intents and purposes, their involvement in the case was now over . . .

'Hang on! Call coming through,' Bill said just as they had attained cruising height on the journey back.

'We've got an emergency up near you.' It was Martin Baird's voice, distorted a little by the equipment.

'Yes?' Clifford replied.

'A road accident. No details. On the Tanama gasfields road, about two kilometres from the Diri Diri turn off.'

Diri Diri! The name sent an instinctive shiver through Janet. But of course Stephanie and Frank weren't there at the moment, and the turn-off was miles from the homestead itself, in any case.

'What about landing?' Bill asked.

169

'Again, no details,' Martin Baird replied. 'I'm suspicious about that call. The guy wouldn't give his name or his call sign. It could be a hoax . . .'

'Or a hit-and-run,' Clifford put in grimly. 'Where are Lance and Paul?'

'South-west sector.'

'Better give them a warning call. They might be needed. We have no idea how many injured, or how serious it is?'

'No. No further information at all.'

With a new hum to the engine, the plane changed its course, heading for the co-ordinates Martin Baird had named.

'We'll do a couple of circles over it. There should be somewhere to land,' Bill said, clearly preparing himself already for what might be a rough and dangerous landing, demanding every ounce of his pilot's skill.

Janet found time for a few minutes regret—her peaceful haven of a room might be hours away now—then she was preparing herself too, shaking off tiredness, inertia, circular thoughts about Clifford . . .

It did not seem long before they began to descend and slow their speed, while Bill and Clifford from their view-point in the front searched the harsh scrub-covered terrain for a sign of the accident.

'That must be it up ahead.' It was Clifford who spoke. 'We've just flown over the Diri Diri turn-off and they said about two miles further on.'

'Looks nasty.' Bill voiced their common thought laconically.

The vehicle looked like a mini-bus from the air, but it lay upside down, and what seemed to be one of its doors was flung completely clear of the wreckage. The road was clear—the mini-bus lay many metres to the side of it—but the terrain on either side had more growth of timber than Bill had evidently expected.

'I'd forgotten it was this kind of country,' he muttered, circling back away from the wrecked vehicle.

'Someone's waving—or at least, I saw some kind of movement,' Janet put in.

'Good work, Janet,' Clifford said, straining his neck now to see. The aircraft was still wheeling around.

'It'll have to be the road,' Bill said.

'Wouldn't the track that joins in on this side be safer?' Clifford asked, more tensely now that they all knew there was definitely someone alive, and probably hurt and trapped, inside the upturned vehicle.

'Less likely to have traffic, but more likely to be rough,' was Bill's comment. 'I'll risk the main road.'

He came in low over it, studying it carefully, then flew out ahead of where the accident had occurred and wheeled around into position.

'Here we go.'

Janet was tight in her seatbelt, gripping its metal buckle with wet hands. She could tell from Bill's manner that the landing was more dangerous than he was letting on. They were skimming over the ground, which she saw only as a racing blur below her. In another second they would be down—But no! With a sudden desperate roar of the engine, Bill had pulled away into the air again, cursing shakily.

'Dirty great erosion gully!' he said when the plane was in control again. 'We'd have gone straight into it. I didn't see it from the other direction, the way the shadows are at the moment.'

He circled again, using up precious seconds which Janet could almost hear ticking by now in the tense atmosphere of the plane.

'I'd better take a closer look this time.'

He skimmed over the ground again and spotted another gully—not deep, but enough to jolt the plane out of all control. Cars on this road would take the ditches very slowly, but a plane as it landed could not.

'Between the two gullies?' Clifford asked.

'Not enough room,' Bill said.

'Surely . . . We can't delay any longer, or afford to look further afield. We could be in the air all day at this rate!' Clifford was not thinking of his own safety, although his voice betrayed the effects of the fear they had all felt during the first failed landing attempt.

Bill was silent for a moment, calculating the risk. Finally he spoke.

'All right. We'll have to try it, I suppose, If I come in right on top of this first gully and brake for all she's worth, we should pull up short of the second one, or at least hit it at a controlled speed—but if we damage the undercarriage . . .'

'We can't afford to,' Clifford said through clenched teeth. 'Go for it.'

For what seemed like the tenth time, they wheeled around the desolate site, coming in so slowly and powerlessly that for a minute Janet was literally holding her breath to keep them airborne. The wheels touched down just feet beyond the first gully and Bill applied the brakes with screaming force, wrestling with the controls to keep the plane from skewing off the road and into the dense, dry scrub.

The breath Janet had held was jerked violently out of her lungs at the first impact of the ground, and then every bone in her body shook. The road was rougher than it looked, and stones bounced up as they slowed, hitting the fuselage with ominous cracks. It seemed as though they would never reach a controlled stop, but at last—and safely—they did.

'A metre short of it, I'd reckon,' Bill said hoarsely.

Janet buried her head in her hands, on the point of nausea. She could not remember ever having been so frightened before, and she had no strength at all . . .

It was Clifford who opened the door of the plane. Seconds later he was at Janet's side, a firm arm around her shoulders.

'Pull yourself together, Janet, there's no time for this.'

The words were firm. It was an instruction not to be

disobeyed, but he didn't seem angry and the reassurance of his tone gave Janet the strength she needed.

'Okay?' he asked.

'All in a day's work,' she laughed shakily, her voice rising above its usual low pitch.

'Good girl.' He gripped her shoulders for a second with his firm brown fingers and Janet got to her feet, willing herself to be unaffected by his nearness.

Then there was time for nothing but their work, as both heard at the same moment a weak but desperate cry from the upturned vehicle twenty metres away. Clifford was there at a run, on his knees and peering into the upside down cabin of the crushed mini-bus. When Janet arrived, he had already taken in the situation, and flung some instructions back at her immediately.

'Tell Bill to call Paul and Lance urgently. There's four injured people here, and our plane will be going to Adelaide.'

Janet was off without waiting to give a reply. Bill had examined the plane for damage and—superficially, at least—there seemed to be none. He was on the radio immediately following her words, pausing only to send up a prayer of thanks that they had refuelled in Charleville.

When Janet returned to the vehicle, Clifford was easing the only conscious passenger—the one who called and waved to them—out of the distorted space. His leg had been trapped by a jagged piece of metal and he had been too shocked to try to move. Janet examined him while Clifford looked at the other three much more seriously injured passengers.

His head had received a nasty knock, and he was bleeding in several places from gashes made by broken glass and twisted metal, but there were no serious injuries. After taking him to the plane, Janet quickly bandaged the worst of his cuts and found the thermos of hot sweet tea they carried. Then she set him temporarily in a sitting position in the back of the plane.

As she worked, he was spilling feverish, garbled details about the accident, which she tried to make sense of, knowing that they might be vital later on.

'The guys didn't even wait,' he said. 'There were two of them, I think. I was asleep just before it happened. I suppose their truck just sped out of that side track without looking. They didn't even hit us but it was definitely their fault. I woke up like lightning but it was all over before I could even realise what was happening. And they didn't even wait.'

'Try to keep still,' Janet put in as he paused. His agitation was making it difficult for her to work on his bleeding cuts.

'When I came to, I just saw this leg in jeans in front of me, stained with dried blood. I suppose it was from the accident, but how did it get on him? I don't know.' He paused for a gulp of tea. 'He said something to his mate about getting out before there was trouble. I think he thought we were all dead, or too far gone to hear him. He didn't notice I had my eyes open. Then his mate came and pulled him away and he staggered a bit. I think he had hurt his left leg in the accident or something. That blood. Anyway, he limped. Maybe he was drunk. I don't know.'

'Perhaps you'd better just stay quiet now,' Janet said at the end of the confused flow. She felt sick to realise that it *was* a hit-and-run as they had suspected when the call came through—and a particularly nasty one at that, with four men lying injured. Radioing the RFDS was the only humane thing the two men had done.

She shivered, too, at the injured man's description of the two 'mates' who, it seemed, had caused the accident. One calling the other to come away before there was trouble. That leg covered in dried blood . . .

Dried blood? But it couldn't have been congealed already if it had happened in the accident—and if the truck hadn't even hit the mini-bus. Janet returned to Clifford's side, but her mind was working hard, jolted by her memory of another leg that had had blood on it . . .

Clifford's face was a mask of anguished concentration. Now an inert form lay on the ground near him, one leg twisted strangely.

'Check the depth of that coma, Janet,' he flung at her.

Janet made the observations as thoroughly as she could. Not good . . . He was a young man, too. Clifford had succeeded in freeing another of the passengers, whose colour and vital signs were much better, if Janet was judging right. Clifford confirmed this.

'Slight head injuries,' he said. 'And a broken collar bone. Nothing internal as far as I can see. Paul can take him and your first one to Broken Hill. These two . . .' he indicated the man on the ground and the last man, who he was now delicately easing from the vehicle, 'are a lot worse.'

Janet was ready with the support he needed, and it did not take much training to see that this one had serious injuries, mainly to the spine.

'We've got to get going straight away,' Clifford was saying. 'We'll need help from Bill with the stretchers.'

'And me. I'm okay now. At least, I want to help.'

It was the injured man, Chris Wade, whom Janet had left in the plane. He was still weak and white, but concern for his friends—it was now evident that they were a group of workers headed back to Tanama gasfields after a few days break—gave him the energy to keep going.

'Bill's preparing a better strip for take-off,' Janet said. 'And he's going to mark it for Lance's landing.'

'Good. Let's hope it doesn't take long.'

Clifford and Janet returned to the plane and brought stretchers, Chris managing to help in spite of his bandages. Both seriously ill patients were loaded into the aircraft by the time Bill returned.

'That side track is better after all,' he said. 'I've removed some branches and set up some rough flags marking it for Lance. We'll ease the plane across

this erosion gully. We'll even be taking off into the
wind!'

'Chris.' Clifford turned to the pale, bandaged man.
'We'll have to leave you here.' Janet saw the man's face
fall.

'No choice, I'm afraid,' Clifford went on. 'Another
plane is on its way to pick up you and your mate. It
should be here at any time, but we've got to get to
Adelaide, or it may be too late.'

The man nodded bleakly and sat in the thin band of
shade cast by the wrecked vehicle, to keep his lonely
vigil.

Janet, absorbed in helping to connect up life support
equipment to the patients in the back of the plane, had
only a moment to reflect again on the loneliness of this
region and the demands it made on its inhabitants. Diri
Diri—stark and desolate itself—was about thirty miles
away to the south-west, and it was probable that the
people there were the nearest living souls to the two
injured men the medical team were leaving behind.

The Piper Chieftain's take-off was, mercifully, far less
dramatic than the landing had been, though the jolting
of the wheels across the rough terrain had Janet and
Clifford—both in the back, cramped and alert—
watching fearfully over their patients. One man was
clinging to life by a thread which might be broken by less
than a few jolts.

Time became unimportant for Janet during the long
journey to Adelaide. All her thoughts were concen-
trated on willing the two patients to stay alive until they
reached Adelaide's most up-to-date Intensive Care
Unit. Bill was in radio contact with Lance as soon as they
were safely airborne, and it seemed that the second
aircraft was about twenty minutes from the accident site.
With Bill's instructions about landing, the transport of
the two less seriously injured patients should be almost
routine.

Landing in Adelaide finally, in the late afternoon, was

a shock to the system. Two ambulances were already positioned as close to the plane as safety allowed on the busy tarmac, and within seconds the two men were transferred into them and on their way, under the care, now, of the ambulance medical crews. Clifford did not even have to give details about their conditions, as this had been done by radio during the journey, so that preparations for receiving the critically injured patients could be made in advance, both in the ambulances and in the Intensive Care Unit of the hospital itself.

It was strange to be standing on the tarmac at Clifford's side watching the two patients speeding away out of her life, Janet thought. She would have no more personal contact with them now, although of course news of their progress would be conveyed regularly to Benanda.

'Will they be all right, I wonder?' She was not even aware that she had spoken the words aloud until Clifford replied after a pause, still watching the ambulances in the distance too.

'Yours should be. Mine . . . won't, I'm afraid.'

'DOA?'

'Yes. It's for the best. He had massive internal injuries. I did what I could, but . . . He'll go without knowing anything about it, fortunately.'

Bill was beside them now, too.

'I've got to move the plane.'

'Move it?' Janet turned to him, confused.

'Yes. We're not flying back tonight. It's too late in the day. We wouldn't get clearance, as it's not an emergency,' Bill explained.

'A hotel, then?' Clifford said.

'I'll stay with my sister,' Bill replied. 'It'll be good to see her. But I'm afraid she wouldn't have room for you too.'

'It's all right,' Janet put in quickly. 'A hotel will be fine.'

'Hop back in the plane and I'll give you a ride over to

the terminal before I park her,' Bill said, and both took up his suggestion quickly, as the airfield, although at a distance from Adelaide's main domestic airport, was still heavily used, and their Piper Chieftain was only in the way now that the emergency was over.

'The other two will be safely at Broken Hill by now, won't they?' Janet asked as they made the short trip across the tarmac. Clifford and Bill both simply nodded briefly, tired after the drama of the day. But thinking of the injured man she had treated reminded Janet of his tangled explanation of the accident.

'Clifford . . .' It seemed natural, somehow, to ask his advice about it.

'Yes?'

'Chris Wade, the conscious man, told me a bit about the accident and he said something . . . It's probably stupid, but it made me think of those two roo-shooters we treated back in January. Ted, and his thigh wound, and the brother Matt.'

Clifford was immediately alert.

'It was them in the other vehicle?' he asked.

'I don't know. It's just an idea.' It sounded foolish and melodramatic now. 'He said that there were two of them, in a truck—which he didn't see, he just heard it revving away, and he said that one came right up and looked in the cabin of the mini-bus. He had a limp in his left-leg—and it was Ted's left leg that was shot—and his pants had dried blood on them, as a roo-shooter's might. I remember noticing that with Matt and Ted.'

Bill whistled softly.

'Those two trouble-makers again.'

'Looks like it,' Clifford said shortly.

'I put two and two together . . . but I might be wrong,' Janet said.

'I don't think so, Janet,' Clifford replied. 'It sounds a very reasonable theory to me, and it's an important step in getting the thing cleared up. There will be a police inquiry, and they'll be very grateful for your information

—unless the pair in the truck come forward and identify themselves before then.'

'Which if it is those two, they won't,' Bill growled. 'They radioed in anonymously, remember? And they can't try and pretend it's because they didn't know how to operate the transceiver properly.'

There was little left to say. Legally, it was in the hands of the police now, and medically, the two hospitals had taken over. It was a funny feeling. Janet voiced this after she and Clifford had left the plane, saying goodbye to Bill and arranging to be back at the aerodrome early in the morning.

'I don't really feel as though I'm in Adelaide,' she said. 'It's like some weird three-dimensional film being projected around me.'

'I know,' Clifford laughed and nodded. 'I've experienced it before.'

'What shall we do? It's only about six, isn't it?'

She could have bitten her tongue out seconds later, realising that it sounded as though she was angling to spend the evening entirely in his company. She went on hastily.

'I mean . . . I've only been to Adelaide once before. I don't know the city at all well . . .'

She stopped. That had only made it worse. It was really impossible, now, for him to abandon her, and he would think she had put on the lost-little-girl act on purpose. She stared at the ground, hot with embarrassment and oblivious to her surroundings. They had passed through the terminal building and were standing outside waiting at a taxi rank.

'Let's not make any decisions until we've found a hotel,' Clifford said, stepping forward as a red and white vehicle pulled up in front of them.

Janet risked a glance at him but could not read his face. They climbed into the back together and he named a hotel which meant nothing to Janet. It could be the most luxurious place in town for all she knew, and she

wondered whether Clifford was happy to make all the
arrangements for them both.

Suddenly, she felt too tired to care, and surrendered
herself to the luxury of sitting back in the taxi and not
even thinking about where they were going.

The city still hummed with the last of the afternoon
peak-hour traffic, the line of hills rising to the east was a
striking mixture of charcoal grey and harvest yellow, and
it was much cooler here so much further south—a
refreshing, invigorating and comfortable temperature
which still allowed short sleeves. The taxi moved
smoothly along the city's tree-lined streets and no one
spoke.

Clifford's long legs were stretched towards the middle
of the vehicle, his cream trouser-leg brushing the tired-
looking cotton of Janet's uniform skirt. He was staring
with passive interest out of the window just as Janet was
doing, and it seemed suddenly very right that they
should be together like this, and inconceivable that
of course he would prefer it if Janet was Stephanie.
Adelaide felt like a different world, a world where the
hostility she was trying to feel for him didn't matter. She
sighed, her careless tranquillity broken by the thought.

'Nearly there.' Clifford had heard the sound and
misinterpreted it. Even as tired as he must be, he was
still alert to the feelings of others.

CHAPTER ELEVEN

'You're lucky. These are the last two rooms,' a reception clerk told them at the desk of a quietly tasteful place in North Adelaide. If he was surprised that two young people who could easily be a couple wanted separate rooms he did not show it.

Clifford took both keys, then led the way to the lift. Their rooms were two flights up. He opened the door for Janet and she was greeted by a leafy view across the River Torrens to the city, and an absolutely inviting bed.

'Janet, you wanted to know about our evening,' Clifford said, surveying the scene. 'How about this: A shower to wash away the desert from your skin, an hour to lie down between those cool white sheets, a long drink somewhere, and a quiet dinner.'

He spoke softly, almost caressingly, and the picture he presented was such an enticing one that Janet just nodded with a dreamy smile and half-closed eyes.

'Perfect!'

'Did you realise that we'd skipped lunch altogether?' he asked.

'I suppose my stomach did,' Janet replied. 'But I don't think my brain is in a fit state to receive the message!'

He left her then, and she did just as he had suggested, slipping naked between the sheets after her shower and not thinking any further ahead than sleep . . . She was woken by a knock and quickly retrieved a towel, her heart sinking as she saw the crumpled and travel-stained uniform she had flung over the back of a chair. She'd have to wear that to dinner. How awful.

Clifford stood at the door—Janet tightened the towel around her, too aware of him as always—and he carried two shopping-bags which he presented to her.

'What . . . ?'

'It was an impulse,' he said, looking boyishly self-conscious all of a sudden. 'I thought of our grotty clothes, and remembered it was late-night shopping night . . . I hope you like them.'

He was gone before she could even thank him, and almost before she had registered that he now wore a soft cream silk shirt and well-tailored dark cord pants. From the bags he had thrust at her, Janet drew out a tunic-style dress in rustling ivory taffeta, a loosely-falling black jacket in the same silky material, and black, low-heeled slippers. He had even got her size right, she realised moments later as she put them on.

'Did I do the right thing?' he asked, appearing again after ten minutes.

'It's all gorgeous, but . . . when did you find time for a rest?'

'I didn't,' he laughed. 'I can't rest at this time of day unless I've been up all night. The rooms have balconies. I sat on mine for fifteen minutes, just drinking in the evening air, and that was enough.'

He was smiling down at her, and Janet had to smile back, though she felt a bit like the little mermaid in the fairy story who was walking on knives underneath her bright exterior.

'It's Festival time here, do you realise?' he was saying.

'Of course! March!' Janet exclaimed. 'I hadn't thought of it.'

'So I booked us into the restaurant at the Festival Theatre Centre. We could walk across, if you'd like to, and look at an open-air art exhibition on our way.'

'Lovely!'

It *was* lovely walking at his side like this. The feeling of belonging there was so strong. It was as they walked across the lawns to the Theatre Centre that Clifford broke the mood.

'Stephanie should be here,' he said, looking about him appreciatively. 'It's the kind of thing she misses. The people, the feeling of life, the art and music . . .'

'Then perhaps this is where she should live,' Janet put in dully, feeling a heavy sinking in her heart. Why had she let herself even begin to enjoy being here with him like this? 'Perhaps she shouldn't stay up in the desert.'

'Oh, she's not going to,' Clifford said cheerfully, and suddenly Janet felt helpless tears welling in her eyes. She was tired, needed food, and it was too hard to hold back her feelings, faced with such evidence of Clifford's lack of care for her. Didn't he even realise he was hurting her? 'She and Frank are going to s . . .'

He broke off, having caught sight of her face as he stepped back to let her pass in front of him up some steps.

'Janet?'

'Yes . . .'

'Are you crying?'

'No.'

'I think you are.'

'Well it's my own business.'

'Perhaps.' He pulled her to him, cradling her head on his shoulder, and she was too weak to resist. Perhaps she should have raked together some pride, but she couldn't. 'Tell me what it is. Are you too tired for this? Would you like a meal in your room.'

His voice was infinitely gentle, as if he were speaking to a child.

'I won't have him thinking I'm so weak and immature,' Janet thought to herself suddenly with a flash of spirit. She pulled away and wiped the hot tears with the back of her hand.

'I'm all right now,' she said briskly. 'But tell me —have you and Stephanie made any definite plans for moving down here together, because with Paul leaving Benanda too, and . . .'

'Me and Stephanie?' he asked, amazed and un-grammatical.

'Yes. If she and Frank have decided to split up, and you think she needs an urban life-style,' Janet said.

'I didn't say they were splitting up.'

'You started to.'

'I started to say they'd decided to sell Diri Diri.' He sounded exasperated. They had both stopped dead on the steps—Clifford one step below, so that his face was almost on a level with Janet's. 'They're staying together. Frank has bought a large vineyard in the Barossa Valley. That's why I talked about Stephanie liking Adelaide. They'll be close enough to come down often, as it's not far, yet Frank will have the farming life he loves. I think it's the best decision they've made yet in their marriage.'

'And so . . . You and Stephanie aren't going to live together, or marry . . .'

'I've never wanted to marry Stephanie, Janet.' He was searching her gaze now, his eyes twinkling. His fingers had found her wrists and encircled them gently. 'Is that what you've been thinking all this time?'

'There've been rumours . . .'

'And would you have minded?' He had bent closer, and his mouth was very near hers. His tone was at once coaxing, teasing, and very gentle. Janet was too mes-merised by his nearness to be anything but honest, and suddenly she knew that honesty was safe after all.

'You know I would have.'

Their lips met, sending darting tongues of feeling through her. His arms were firm and they encircled her. His hair was thick and smooth to her caressing fingers. It was the unbelievable moment she had been waiting for for so long. People might have been watching them. They didn't care . . .

'Janet?' Clifford said, breaking off ages later.

'Yes, Clifford?'

'Do you love me?'

'Yes.'

'I wonder why it took us so long to find out.'

'Perhaps we should discuss it over dinner.'

'Hungry?'

'Very!'

'I was a fool not to realise that you thought I was involved with Stephanie, and that was why you rejected me,' Clifford said when they were seated in an intimate corner of the restaurant, cool, creamy brandy alexanders waiting in front of them.

'You were involved with her at one time, weren't you?' Janet asked hesitantly. 'Paul said so . . .'

'That was over two years ago in Sydney,' Clifford said, speaking softly—his words, and his eyes, only for Janet. 'I'd already applied for the job at Benanda. We went out together for a while. It was through me that she met Frank. When they fell in love I was piqued, I admit. It was then that I decided I must have loved her, but it was only hurt pride, and I realised that soon enough.'

'Paul said you had gone to Benanda especially to be with her,' Janet said.

'Gossip often gets things wrong, my darling.'

'And yet . . . Stephanie was in love with you. I know she was,' Janet frowned, taking the caressing hand Clifford held out to her across the table and leaning towards him. 'When she stayed at your place on her way back up to Diri Diri . . .'

'Stephanie was very scared,' Clifford said. 'She's just not made to live in the outback. It *is* a different life, very different, from the city. You know that, and you can cope with it. You know the stresses and the rewards. Stephanie only knows the stresses, and can't handle them. She had a nervous breakdown last spring . . .'

'Yes, I'd heard a bit about that.'

'And she went south to her family in Sydney. I thought she should have stayed there throughout the summer, and then come back to Frank with the aim of working out a compromise together. She does love him.

They complement each other in the right ways when Stephanie is at her best. You haven't seen that, Janet. She came back to the region too soon, and at the height of the hot weather when the country is at its most desolate. I think she realised that as soon as she arrived at Benanda. She turned to me out of desperation, as she had done before, during her breakdown, tricking herself out of fear into believing she loved me and her marriage had been a mistake. Frank was jealous and suspicious. His asthma got worse. He started to believe there had been more in our relationship than there ever was. I couldn't help feeling partly responsible for what was happening and it concerned me a lot. Now that they've started to sort out their lives, I feel so much better. But when Frank was feeling insecure and wasn't sure that she would stay with him . . . You came into the middle of some of that tension that first day at Diri Diri on the clinic flight.'

'I remember it,' Janet nodded.

'I wanted to explain it to you then, but out of a sense of privacy and concern for Frank and Stephanie, I felt . . .'

'It doesn't matter,' she assured him.

'And yet if I *had* explained, we might have avoided all this misunderstanding,' Clifford frowned. 'I was attracted to you already even then, but I was too caught up in worrying over Stephanie and Frank, and I didn't know where Paul fitted in. I pictured you as a shallow thoughtless flirt before you even arrived at Benanda . . .'

'Because you thought I'd come up to be with Paul?'

'Yes. I didn't realise that you knew the region . . . Seeing you with that hair—even though it was glorious, and that first afternoon at Broken Hill airport I wanted to run my fingers through it and press it to my face . . .'

'Really? I didn't guess.' She leaned forward, and he kissed her with tantalising softness.

'But I knew it wasn't practical. It only confirmed my belief that you didn't know what you were letting yourself in for.'

'I'd thought about my hair, but I couldn't bear to part with it. I was wrong.'

'I love it now.'

'You helped a lot when I had to cut it.'

'Did I?'

'Maybe that's why I fell in love with you.'

'I was confused about you for far too long. Did you want Paul? Was my feeling just physical? It was that night at Moollawindra when I realised what I wanted from you. But I didn't know why you responded then turned cold. I felt elated and cast down by turns, depending on how you looked at me. This morning for example, I was feeling good about Stephanie and Frank's decision, and I started to think you might care, but then later . . . I know now it was all because of what you thought about Stephanie.'

'And there was Marcia.'

'Marcia Fairfax?'

'Yes. You flirted with her. Don't try to deny it!' Janet could afford to tease and scold him now.

'Perhaps I did,' he admitted. 'She's fun to be with. But she's too young. She doesn't want to settle down yet, and I certainly wouldn't want to settle down with her!'

'I realised that—but only after Stephanie's suicide attempt, that evening when I was at your place and Marcia came round . . .'

'Only then? I wanted to tell you I loved you that night, find out what exactly you did think about me and Stephanie and Frank, and why you were so angry. I guessed in part from what you said, but I didn't realise you thought a divorce was in the wind. When you brushed me off I thought you couldn't love me, yet I couldn't believe that.'

'I listened too much to what everyone else was saying,

not what my heart said, and your eyes . . .' Janet replied.

'Your eyes are beautiful . . .'

There was a pause as he kissed her again, making melting tingles course inside her, and her body long for closer contact. A waiter interrupted them with a discreet cough, and laid steaming entrées of ham and asparagus crêpes in front of them.

'Can we go on living at Benanda?' Clifford asked Janet, serious again now.

'Why not?'

'It's a harsh region . . .'

'I know that.'

'The violence, the cruelty of nature in that climate, the isolation . . .'

'But that's why I want to stay,' Janet said earnestly. 'Because our work is helping so much to break that isolation. That's where the reward is—to know that without the RFDS all of those men today could well have died—and probably those two malnourished children as well. Helping people like Frank and Stephanie, too. Perhaps we won't stay there forever, but for the next few years . . .'

'Till our children start school?'

'Till then,' she nodded, laughing at him with eyes of love.

'Do you think we've sorted out everything?' he asked her. 'No more doubts?'

'No more doubts,' she replied. 'Plenty more to talk about and discover . . .'

'And discover . . . Eat your meal,' he commanded suddenly, reaching out a hand to caress the soft line of her jaw and throat in a way that made Janet want to catch at the hand and cover it with exploring kisses. 'I'd like to get on with some of that discovering later tonight . . . And I have the feeling that one of our hotel rooms may prove superfluous for the purpose, don't you think?'

'That thought had crossed my mind, yes.'
'What a pity we have to get up so early in the morning,
my darling . . .'

 **Harlequin Romance**

Coming Next Month

2953   BLIND TO LOVE   Rebecca Winters
When Libby Anson joins her husband in Kenya, she's shocked
by his announcement that their marriage is over. He insists that
his blindness changes everything. But it doesn't—not for Libby.

2954   FETTERS OF GOLD   Jane Donnelly
Nic is in love with Dinah. Although Dinah isn't as sure of her
feelings for Nick, there's no way she'll let his overbearing
cousin Marcus dictate what they can or cannot do!

2955   UNEXPECTED INHERITANCE   Margaret Mayo
Alice is far from delighted at the prospect of a visit to the
West Indies, all expenses paid. It means giving in to the
commands of her unknown grandfather's will. Worse still, it
means seeing Jared Duvall again....

2956   WHEN TWO PATHS MEET   Betty Neels
Katherine is properly grateful to Dr. Jason Fitzroy for rescuing
her from the drudgery of her brother's household and helping
her to find a new life-style. She can't help dreaming about him,
though she's sure he's just being kind.

2957   THE CINDERELLA TRAP   Kate Walker
Dynamic Matt Highland doesn't connect the stunning model
Clea with the plump unattractive teenager he'd snubbed years
ago. But Clea hasn't forgotten—or forgiven—and she devises a
plan to get even!

2958   DEVIL MOON   Margaret Way
Career girl Sara is a survivor in the jungle of the television
world, but survival in the real jungle is a different matter, as she
finds out when her plane crashes. There, she is dependent on
masterful Guy Trenton to lead the party to safety....

Available in January wherever paperback books are sold, or
through Harlequin Reader Service:

In the U.S.
901 Fuhrmann Blvd.
P.O. Box 1397
Buffalo, N.Y. 14240-1397

In Canada
P.O. Box 603
Fort Erie, Ontario
L2A 5X3

Harlequin Historicals

Step into a world of pulsing adventure, gripping emotion and lush sensuality with these evocative love stories penned by today's best-selling authors in the highest romantic tradition. Pursuing their passionate dreams against a backdrop of the past's most colorful and dramatic moments, our vibrant heroines and dashing heroes will make history come alive for you.

Watch for two new Harlequin Historicals each month, available wherever Harlequin books are sold. History was never so much fun—you won't want to miss a single moment!